ALPHA
UNBOUND

Feral Pack: Book One

EVE LANGLAIS

Copyright © 2021 /2022 Eve Langlais

Cover by Joolz & Jarling (Julie Nicholls & Uwe Jarling) © 2021/2022

Produced in Canada

Published by Eve Langlais

http://www.EveLanglais.com

Canadian Intellectual Property Office Registration Number : 1181947

E-ISBN: 978 1 77 384 254 7

Print ISBN: 978 1 77 384 255 4

ONE

"Someone pissed on the raspberries by the northern pasture fence." Amarok had noticed it during a walk of the property.

"No. Not the raspberries." Darian sounded most put out. Everyone on the ranch knew he'd been keeping an eye on the patch, waiting for them to ripen. They'd gotten a late start due to a delayed spring and summer. Now ticking into fall, the last time anyone checked they'd been a dark pink, almost ready for picking.

No one was missing out on Poppy's raspberry upside-down cake. Or her saliva-inducing tarts. Good thing Amarok exercised a lot since she'd arrived and spoiled them with excellent cooking.

Hopping off the railing, Asher, the troublemaker with his easy grin, spread his hands. "Bah, it's only piss. No big deal. Just rinse them off. Can't be any worse than you licking your balls."

The scowl Darian bestowed should have shriveled Asher on the spot. "Not all of us are pervs."

"It's natural. All of the animals do it. At least the clean ones who enjoy getting laid. When was the last time for you?" Asher pretended to think for a second before exclaiming, "A long time. Now explained by your refusal to tongue your genitals."

Before it could devolve into a fight, Amarok—current owner of said raspberry patch and the three hundred plus acres around it—frowned. "If you're gonna fight, take it somewhere there's no plants. Astra said she'd skin the next person who trampled any of them."

A warning meted out while she sharpened her knife. Only an idiot would peeve the very pregnant and hormonal Astra.

"Is she watching?" Asher turned a fearful gaze behind him. Having had his hair shorn for trimming a bush because its branches were tickling his car, he knew better than to touch a single leaf on any of her plants.

"She's always watching," Amarok grumbled. But good-naturedly.

Astra was like a sister to them. As were Poppy

and Nova, despite the fact they shared no blood. At the ranch, family was the people you trusted.

"Back to the piss. Any ideas who did it?" Amarok asked. Not one of them, and not only because they knew each other's scent. No one living at White Wolf Ranch—the name his uncle gave it when Amarok moved in as a teen—would do such a dick thing.

"Odd spot for a hiker to get lost," Asher remarked.

The ranch was so far off the beaten track that no one ever came out here. The rumors of wolves in these parts helped, too.

"Whatever pissed contaminated the scent with asparagus," Amarok growled.

Asher gagged. "Oh, gross." Everyone knew its pungent effect on urine.

It indicated planning, which raised Darian's brows. "Are the bears testing our borders again?" They'd had a problem last year with a few wild ursine looking to expand their territory.

They learned their lesson quickly when the wolves that kept hikers away chased them well past their boundaries.

"Could be," Amarok conceded. "Although the asparagus would indicate they're raiding someone's garden. I don't know of any in the area other than ours, and we don't grow that nasty shit." Because none of them could stand the smell of their pee after.

"What about tracks?"

"It's the weirdest fucking thing." Darian shook his head. "Whoever pissed somehow covered their tracks into the patch and out."

Which meant the marking was a message. A warning, perhaps, but from whom?

Standing by the bay window in the living room, Asher randomly remarked, "Did Big Betty give birth?" Big Betty being the name for their diesel Ford truck painted a bright cherry red with one fat white stripe slashed horizontally across its middle.

"What the fuck are you talking about?" Amarok glanced out the window. A modern hybrid car was parked in his driveway. It was a small two-door, the same hue as his work truck, and so silent he had not heard it pulling up the road to the house.

"Who the fuck is crazy enough to drive one of those out here?" Darian gaped. With good reason. They didn't live in a civilized area of Northern Alberta. "That thing meets a bison or a moose and it's scrap metal."

No shit. Then again, pretty much nothing could survive impact with any of the wild animals roaming this area.

"How many hamsters do you think it has

running under the hood?" Asher never took shit seriously.

"Not many, considering the driver is tiny."

Indeed, the woman exiting the car couldn't have been more than five feet, maybe a few inches over. Shapely, though. Her jeans hugged rounded hips, and her T-shirt clung to her tits. Nice tits, Amarok should add. He'd know. At thirty-three, he'd stared at his fair share. Bitten and licked more than a few, too.

"Anyone know who she is?" Darian asked.

They didn't get visitors often at the ranch. Lonely country road in the middle of fucking nowhere—just the way they liked it. Forty minutes from the nearest town, if you could call Fort Mackay a town. Since oil went bust in Alberta, shattering the economy in the north, there were more shuttered businesses than open.

"She's cute." Asher finger combed his hair.

"She's a stranger," grumbled Amarok.

She carried a binder, leading Darian to ask, "Think she's one of them Jehovah's?"

"Oh, hell yeah. I'll take care of her." Asher's expression brightened. He began tugging at his shirt. His idea of dealing with religious doorknockers was to strip naked and ask them if they wanted to commune with him in nature.

Amarok—who his friends called Rok—had

thought them done with pushy evangelists and others. What part about no soliciting did they not grasp? He lived in the middle of nowhere. It was ridiculous.

"I'll handle this," he stated as the petite woman climbed the steps to the sprawling ranch house. Originally owned by his uncle, Rok had inherited the place as the only remaining family.

Rok flung open the door before she could knock and almost slammed it shut as her scent hit him like a slug to the gut.

Mine.

TWO

SUCH A NICE, SUNNY MORNING. MEADOW GOT TO see it in all its glory on the drive to White Wolf Ranch, a gorgeous place set in the woods. The air was fragrant the moment she stepped out of her car. Pine and green stuff growing. Which her mom said wasn't a description and yet it summed it up perfectly for Meadow.

Bees hummed. Branches creaked. The noises of nature. She felt utterly at peace and couldn't help but smile with happiness as the door to the house opened before she could even knock.

Startled, she clung tight to her binder and chirped, "Hi. How are you? Me, I'm feeling pretty darned good. This place is absolutely marvelous."

"What do you want?" snarled a beautiful man with eyes the most stunning color of amber, which she saw only because she craned. He towered over her, which wasn't hard to do. He scowled, quite formidably, not that it detracted from his attractiveness.

She'd never truly grasped the term dumbstruck until now, which led to her babbling. "Are you psychic?"

He blinked. Sinfully long dark lashes as silky looking as his hair, which was pulled back from a face with sharp features. "What?"

"You must be psychic. You opened the door as if you just knew I'd be there." She beamed. Could this meeting be karma?

His displeasure deepened. "It's called a fucking window. I saw you getting out of your car. If you can call that thing a car." His disparagement was clear.

But Meadow had been fielding that attitude since she bought it. "Isn't it adorable? That's part of the reason I bought it, but it's got more than just cuteness going for it. I never have trouble parking, and you wouldn't believe how cheap it is to run!"

"Because you tuck it in your purse and carry it?" he drawled.

She laughed. "You're funny."

That only had him grimacing more fiercely. "I'm not funny, nor are cars supposed to be adorable."

"You must be a truck guy." She bobbed her head.

One thing she'd learned since leaving the familiar confines of the city was just how many people owned big gas guzzlers.

He leaned against the doorjamb. "Yup. Big fucking V8 that could fit two of your toy cars in the back."

"Guess a truck would be a little more practical given this is a real ranch."

"As opposed to?"

"A fake one."

"I don't even want to know. Are you ever going to get to the point? What do you want?"

"I would love to have a word with the owner of the property, please." According to her research, it used to be Tomas Silla, but when he passed, he left it to his nephew, Amarok Fleetfoot, who had absolutely no online presence.

"Why?"

"I have something of great importance to discuss with him." She clung to the edges of her binder and rolled on the balls of her feet. She'd taken a big risk driving out here when she couldn't find a phone number or email contact.

"Did one of the ranch hands knock you up?"

Her mouth rounded in surprise. "No." But the mere fact he asked? "Does that happen often?"

Rather than reply, he had a new question. "Are you selling farm equipment or supplies?"

"No, I—"

"Then we have nothing to talk about." He went to close the door, but she'd not driven this far to give up that easily.

"Please, hear me out."

"I'm not interested in your sales pitch."

"No sale pitch, more like a request. And a harmless one, I swear. Won't cost you a thing."

"Not interested."

"But you haven't even heard me out." She didn't mean to pout, but her lower lip did jut, and his gaze flicked to it.

"Doesn't matter what you want. The answer is no."

Spoken in a firm tone that indicated he meant it, but Meadow was determined. "I swear I won't interfere with you or your ranch. I just need access to the creek running through your property." She finally drew his full attention.

"Why?"

"Because of Weaver." She hurried to explain. "Weaver is a very rare albino beaver I've been studying and documenting since his birth inside a sanctuary. He was recently fitted with a tracker and released into the wild, which was terrifying. He was raised in captivity. He's not like other beavers."

"Does he chew wood?"

"He did when he was in our care, but now that he's free, we have no idea what he's doing. Not to mention, his coloring makes him stand out. Given how special he is, I'd like to document his progress, which I can only do with your permission since his tracker shows him having chosen your land as his home."

"If he made it here, then it sounds as if he's doing just fine."

"If it is him. Could be something ate his tracker." She hated saying it, but she had to know.

"He's not dead."

"You've seen him?"

He didn't reply, but she could tell.

She clapped her hands. "That's amazing. If could just have a few days to look? Maybe—"

"No."

"But—"

"N. O."

The door slammed in her face.

THREE

Asher, who'd been standing to the side listening the entire time, burst out laughing. "Dude, I can't believe that just happened."

Him either. Who the fuck showed up unannounced to ask if they could spy on his land? Document his ass. Even if the little lady spoke true, like fuck. The ranch was a safe place for his kind. Weres. Not one for humans. Although the beaver could stay.

"She's still here," Asher whispered suddenly.

Rok already knew. He could feel her on the other side. Didn't like it one bit. The moment he'd opened that door he'd been hyper aware of her—practically drooled at her scent, orange citrus shampoo and motel soap. She was pretty up close. Mid to late twenties. Hair wild with natural curl. Finger bare. But that didn't mean shit these days.

"Why isn't she leaving?" Asher continued to whisper.

They got their answer a moment later as a scrap of paper slid under the door. They all stood there staring at it as if it might explode if they touched it.

All fucking dumbasses. Scared of a little human woman. Amarok snared it from the floor and read the message.

In case you change your mind. She'd included a website address along with a phone number. But the thing that had him balling it up and tossing it into the fireplace? The fucking happy face she drew.

He glanced out the window to see her getting back into her clown car. Since the road only went one place, she'd end up back in town. Good.

She didn't know what she asked. Letting a human, even a cute and tiny one, poke her nose around his woods wasn't a good idea. He owned this ranch for a reason, and it wasn't because it made good money. It didn't. Or because he liked farming. He fucking hated it. But he loved this place. The only place he'd ever lived and been happy. He had his uncle to thank for that.

Tossed out of his pack at sixteen, he'd been homeless. A lone wolf was rarely welcomed by other groups, especially a boy with Alpha tendencies. The rejection didn't really bother him since he had no interest in following anyone's rules but his own.

But living on the streets quickly lost its allure. Desperate, he remembered a letter he'd gotten as a boy. From his mother's brother. Inviting him to visit anytime. His father refused. A sixteen-year-old on the streets had nothing to lose. It turned out to be the best thing he ever did.

"I'm going for a walk." Rok remained in is two-legged shape for it, his long, easy stride taking him to the creek and the recently constructed beaver dam. Spotting it brought her to mind, and he growled.

Why couldn't he get her out of his head? He stripped and ran. A good hard panting sprint that eased some of the tension. Until he got home. The moment he hit his porch, he'd have sworn he scented her still.

Fuck.

He eschewed the front door for the back and stalked inside and snared some clothes out of a basket kept there for just that reason. The mudroom with laundry led to the kitchen, where Poppy, Darian's sister, cooked at the stove.

"Who pissed in your coffee?" she asked, stirring the giant pot of soup. The twelve-burner stove held two giant cauldrons, and the oven was roasting meat and potatoes judging by the smell. Almost dinnertime.

"Actually, it was Darian's raspberries that got peed on." He didn't yell at Poppy. No one did. She'd come to the ranch along with her brother a few years ago, the pair of them shadow eyed and serious. Like him, they'd had nowhere to go.

"I heard. He is so pissed." She seasoned a pot before turning to eye him. "Heard we had another visitor today."

"You don't have to worry," he soothed.

"I wasn't." She claimed it, and yet she sometimes flinched if someone knocked at the door or the lights flickered. Poppy might deny it, but in her head, the nightmare hadn't ended.

"You missed the city chick wanting to take selfies with our new resident beaver," he told her, taking a spot at the counter and reaching for a cookie under the dome. Poppy always had something fresh for them to nibble on.

"The white one?"

"You've seen it?"

She nodded. "He's been busy."

Meaning the critter was doing well for the moment, but that could change. These woods were wild. Untamed. Dangerous. Like the people living here. They all had their stories. Their very grimness bound them together.

Dinner proved to be a raucous affair, as it always was every night in the massive dining room. The ranch didn't just come with land and a house. It also had people his uncle had gathered. People like Rok who didn't fit anywhere else.

After the cleanup, Asher said, "Anyone in the mood to line dance and drink shitty beer?"

No and no, but there was one more thing Amarok could get in town. "I'm in. Just let me shower first." Freshly showered men tended to have better prospects with the ladies than the scruffy, drunk ones. It wasn't long before Amarok piled into Big Betty with Asher and Hammer.

Asher had been kicked out of his pack for the sole crime of being a single male, and while he didn't have alpha tendencies, he was popular with the ladies. Too popular. Hammer came to them because he let his fists do the talking one time too many. In his defense, he had a low tolerance for bullshit. So did most of the people at his ranch.

The drive to town was a long one, but sometimes a man needed to get out of his space and blow off some steam. A bar provided the perfect respite. He already knew Asher wouldn't be drinking. The man, for all his light-hearted nature, never did. No booze.

No drugs. No one knew why, and they respected his privacy enough to not ask.

The closest bar, and the one of choice given their limited options, was across the highway from a lodge that could get busy depending on what hunting season it was. Even in the off times the tavern hopped at night. Unemployment checks didn't just pay rent and buy food for the men left behind when the jobs ran dry. Not to mention, there wasn't much else to do.

Seeing the parking lot full of trucks and ATVS, it occurred to Rok he wasn't feeling particularly social. Maybe he should have stayed home. Then again, the tension in him needed release, the kind found between a pair of willing thighs. There weren't many options in a town where men outnumbered women by a ridiculous amount. But in good news, a guy like Rok never had problems getting someone to ease his needs. Maybe Patsy would be working the bar tonight. She was always up for a quick pounding in the backroom.

Upon entering the bar, the noise hit him in a wave. Country music. Loud voices that would get louder the more the beer flowed. The *thwack* of pool cues against balls. The televisions playing constant sports were the only things muted.

Norman was manning the bar. Seeing Rok, the big bald man nodded and filled a mug from the tap.

While Asher went looking for newbies to fleece at billiards, Rok and Hammer found a table in the back. Since facing the room would lead to people either thinking they could chat, or braggarts wanting to challenge, he made a statement by sitting with his back to the door. It wasn't as if anyone could sneak up on him.

He nursed a beer. Checked out the room. Saw a few women he'd slept with before, even a pair of out-of-towners that would do. None of them really appealed, though. He'd need more beer. Or a different woman...

Unbidden—and unwanted—he couldn't help picturing the little lady from earlier. Perfectly shaped. But her scent...it screamed danger.

He knew it the moment she entered. Almost choked on his sip of beer as his whole body jolted to attention. It was more than scent. More than being aware of his surroundings and those in it.

Within, something primal—and terrifying —unfurled.

A certainty.

Mine.

Go to her.

Like fuck. He chugged his mug and choked

when Asher slapped his back with a drawled, "Don't look now, but hamster girl is here."

"Hamster girl?" The name caused Hammer to chuckle.

Rok poured more beer from the pitcher into his glass. It was home brewed and stronger than the stuff bought in a can or bottle. To get really drunk he'd need hard liquor, but he preferred the nicer buzz as opposed to the ugly that came from swigging whiskey.

His dad drank the amber devil, and Rok still remembered the aftermath. His teachers thought he was the clumsiest kid growing up because of course he lied about the bruises. Everyone knew foster care was worst, especially for mixed kids like Rok.

"Is it true? She wanted to study a beaver?" Hammer's query held a note of incredulity.

"I'd study her beaver." A comment Asher had made thousands of times before, and yet, in this instance, Rok took offense.

"Watch your mouth," he snapped.

Asher lifted a brow. "I didn't realize she was spoken for."

"She's not. Just stay away from her. She's trouble." His gut said so, and he always trusted it. It had saved him more times than he could count.

"If by trouble you mean the kind of woman to

make a man think of settling down. I don't think she's the casual type," Hammer opined.

"Meaning not our type at all, eh, boys!" Asher slapped his hand on the table. "I'm gonna go and see if those city slickers brought anything fun with them." Asher loved sharking those who came here with their expensive gear to go hunting and fishing in the wilds. Rok might have interfered except for the fact Asher never fleeced them too much. Nor was he a dick about it. Won a hundred dollars playing pool? He bought a round. Score a bag of weed? The joint went around.

When Hammer left to play darts, Rok almost switched seats, which would have given him a direct line on hamster girl. A horrible nickname for someone so delicate. Someone who really shouldn't be in this type of bar. Then again, what did he know? He'd spoken to her for a minute. Could be he got her all wrong and she was here to party.

It took more will power than it should have to resist the temptation to look, but eventually, when nature called, his head swiveled as he rose. Right away his gaze zoned in on her tucked at the end of the bar, munching on some fries and a burger, a clear fizzy drink by her side.

For a second her gaze met his, as if she'd known

when to look. Their eyes locked. Hers widened as her lips parted and then curved into a smile that hit him below the belt.

He replied with a grimace. The urge within that wanted him to go to her could fuck right off.

Not his type. Too happy for one. Too short for two. And he was sure he could think of more reasons. He broke off their staring match and headed for the bathroom to break the seal. It was easy to forget about a woman when standing at a urinal trough that stank, the walls scrawled with missives.

For a good time call...

Joe's mom is a whore.

Fuck solar.

And then one that caused him to freeze mid-shake.

Who's afraid of the big bad wolf? Then in a violent scrawl. *I'm coming for your pack.*

Probably nothing. Amarok and his ranch crew weren't an official pack, just a bunch of misfit wolves who happened to live in the same place. No legal status with the Lykosium, the group that monitored all things Were. A group he avoided because he knew they wouldn't be pleased about the number of loners gathered in one place.

Was he being watched?

Most likely he was overthinking shit. Probably some hunter, drunk and excited about a planned expedition. After all, it was legal to shoot wolves, which was why during that part of the season they all knew to stick to their grounds and only go out on four feet at night.

Rok washed his hand and dried them on his pants, grimacing at the wet marks on the denim. Fucking bar could at least install blowers given they weren't good about refilling the paper towels. Too many fucktards using them to clog toilets and the urinal.

Exiting the bathroom, he thought about calling it a night. Asher and Hammer could keep the truck. He'd stuff his shit inside and head home on four feet. It wouldn't be the first time.

A glance that was less than casual showed the beaver lady flanked by Wes and Bowie, good-looking local boys, or so the women claimed. But that was on the outside. Inside, they were pure trash. The kind he'd punched out before when they got handsy with Nova. Not that Nova couldn't handle herself. She'd taken care of one while Rok beat the shit of the other. Only when they were crawling away, crying for their mommas, did he warn them, *"Touch any of my friends and next time they won't find your body 'til spring."*

The little lady wasn't his friend.

She was nobody.

Explain why, then, his stride took him to the end of the bar in time to hear her politely but firmly decline their invite to go somewhere private.

"No thank you. It's really nice of you to offer, but I need to get to bed early for work."

"We can go to bed," cajoled Wes.

"We just won't sleep," Bowie added, hooking his thumbs through his belt loops. "We'll tag team you all night long."

She shook her head. "Sorry. I'm not into that kind of thing."

"Only because you haven't tried. You'll have fun. Promise." Wes wouldn't let up and hemmed her in close enough that Rok could see the discomfort on her face.

They took away her smile, which really bothered him for some reason.

Leave it alone. Norman would handle it. The barkeep wasn't one to let women be harassed. But the guy was at the far end, and no one was listening to her polite refusal.

Once more, Rok had no control over himself. "You heard the lady, she said no. So fuck off." His voice was low. Firm. And despite the music, they heard.

Their heads swiveled. Wes snapped, "You fuck off!"

Amarok grinned. "Hello, boys, remember me?"

Judging by their blanched expressions, they did. Bowie backed away first. "We didn't know she was from the ranch."

"She's not." A dumb thing to admit given his interference.

"I'm afraid Mr. Fleetfoot won't let me study his beaver." A guileless reply that almost had him rolling his eyes, especially since it led to Wes and Bowie snickering.

"His beaver, eh? Always thought he looked girly with that long hair." Wes snorted. His own pate was shaved down to hide the signs of balding.

Just one slap. One. His fingers itched.

But his rescue came from elsewhere with a pert, "Only the ruggedly handsome can carry it off." She eyed Bowie with his shaggy waves of hair. "I wouldn't advise it."

It was elegantly done. She took a sip of her drink while Bowie turned red.

While her head was bent, Rok mouthed, *Fuck off.*

The two dicks, who really should think about relocating before their bodies were discovered after a snow melt—tragic accident—moved away to harass someone else. Before Rok could leave as well, she turned a smile on him that sucker-punched his dick.

"Thanks for helping me out there. They really were persistent."

"We don't often get new folks around. Especially pretty female ones."

"Thank you." She blushed.

He scowled. He shouldn't have said pretty. He wasn't trying to flirt. "You should be careful. Some of these guys don't take no for an answer."

"And some know how to use it all too well."

For some reason, the smartass reply made him grin. "Never was a yes man."

"I take it your sudden interest in my presence isn't about changing your mind?"

"No."

"I don't suppose you could explain why? I really wouldn't get in the way. A few weeks of me studying Weaver, taking pictures, and I'd be gone. I promise you wouldn't even know I was there."

He highly doubted that. "It's not safe in the woods."

"Because of the bears. I know. I have a bell."

He blinked. "What's a fucking bell supposed to do?"

"You ring it, and it scares them off."

His jaw just about hit the floor—and almost

didn't recover given the filth. "What fucking moron told you that?"

She gnawed her lower lip, tempting him something fierce. "The guy at the sporting goods store assured me it was the thing to have. And I saw a few videos."

"A tiny bell ain't scaring off a grizzly. Even if it could, it won't do shit for wolves."

More sucking on that lower lip had him almost growling. Did she realize what kind of invitation that sent?

"Are they active in these parts? Have you had attacks?"

"Yes." Mostly because the ranch raised animals they could safely hunt. Being a shifter meant enjoying a fresh kill from time to time. "The woods are dangerous."

"Oh." Such a small sound.

He felt like the biggest cur for wiping her smile. Still, it had to be done. He didn't need a cute little human poking her nose where she shouldn't.

He threw her a bone. "Tell you what. If it makes you feel better, I'll keep an eye on your albino beaver."

"Will he be safe with all those wolves and bears around? He doesn't have the same camouflage as others. How will he hide?" She sounded genuinely worried.

With good reason. "Only the strong survive."

He didn't realize he said it aloud until she stood, barely reaching his chin, and frostily said, "I see. I'm sorry to have wasted your time. Good evening, sir."

And then she walked out.

FOUR

Meadow positively simmered.

What a rude man.

Only the strong will survive, indeed.

So much for being her hero and sending those pushy guys packing. Amarok Fleetfoot remained just as prickly as before. Just as sexy. But he wasn't the one offering to take her to bed.

She sighed. Apparently, she'd wasted her time coming here. She'd set out with such high hopes, too. Had programmed the most epic playlist of songs for the road trip. Brought tons of snacks and drinks. Gotten some lovely images on the way and admired the beauty of her province. So not a total waste!

Her ill humor eased. She might not have gotten to see Weaver, but she'd enjoyed the drive and would take her time going back, seeing the sights. Given

Amarok's adamancy, there was no point in staying. In the morning she'd filled up her car, a delicate process her best friend called Extreme Tetris. She might have a point, given Meadow made judicious use of every spare inch of space, including the passenger seat.

At least Valencia would be happy. Her best friend had argued against her coming here.

"That's mountain man territory! You're so tiny they're liable to toss you over a shoulder and run off with you to their cave."

Valencia might be right about the first part. There was definitely something wild and untamed about Mr. Fleetfoot. A predatory look in his eyes. A strength in his body that clothes couldn't hide. Meadow usually didn't pay much attention to someone's looks, but there was something about him that made her want to openly admire.

Whatever she felt, it wouldn't go anywhere. Tomorrow she'd return to her job at the sanctuary. Her blog on Weaver would see its last update. So much for making a documentary about the cute beaver that stole her heart.

The parking lot was full of trucks, the neon light of the bar flashing erratically. She hugged herself and stayed to the wide-open areas. This place did have rougher sorts than she was used to. Those two men

Mr. Fleetfoot scared off had been pushy. Pushier than she usually had to deal with.

The lodge wasn't far, part of the reason she'd come to the bar to eat. The restaurant inside the place she was staying turned her stomach with its mounted heads and the stuffed animals used as decor. Real ones, not the plush, squishy kind that she sometimes slept with for something to hug.

The noise of the bar spilled into the parking lot and didn't fade until she'd crossed the road. It made the scuff of a step behind her noticeable, and she shivered. Probably just someone else heading to their room.

Her steps quickened. It didn't matter. She found herself suddenly flanked by the very same men Mr. Fleetfoot had chased off.

"Hey there, beaver girl."

She did her best to not show fear. "What a coincidence. Are you staying at the lodge, too?"

"We are now."

Her blood chilled, but she didn't let them daunt her. They were in public. She'd had defense lessons —Valencia insisted she take them, calling Meadow too gullible.

"It's a lovely place. The staff is so kind." At least the woman at the front desk was. Although now she had to wonder why that woman stressed she'd placed her in a room with a deadbolt. Perhaps she should have ordered room service.

The lodge's front entrance wasn't far. She would be fine. The grip on her arm steering her to the left indicated otherwise.

Her heart thumped. Raised to use her words and stand up for herself, she said with only a hint of a tremor, "Please, let go. I'm not comfortable with this."

"We'll have you feeling good real soon. Relax."

"I said no." She tugged. The beginnings of panic hit.

"Calm down. Here. Have a pop of this."

"I don't—"

The bigger of the two held her while the other thrust something into her mouth. Acrid on her tongue, it melted right away. She did her best to spit it out, but already she felt herself getting sluggish.

"What did you do?" she slurred.

"Just loosening you up for the big event," was the chuckled reply.

When he tried to kiss her, she roused enough to yell. "No. Stop. Help!"

A hand clapped over her mouth, cutting off all sound. She found herself tossed over a shoulder just like Valencia predicted!

But before the brute could take her to his cave,

she heard a low voice. "What the fuck do you think you're doing?"

She was abruptly dumped on the ground. She blinked heavy lids and tried to make sense of the commotion. Meaty thuds. Whimpering. Then nothing.

She lay on the ground, trying to stay awake and failing.

The handsome Mr. Fleetfoot crouched over her. At his scowl, she managed a smile. "My hero." Then fell asleep.

FIVE

WHAT THE FUCK?

Amarok stared at the sleeping little lady and wanted to curse a bit longer. A good thing he'd decided to follow her to make sure she ended up back at her hotel safe. Although he'd spent a minute longer arguing with himself about it than he should have, which was why he arrived as Dead and Deader were already leading her away. To add to their heinous crime, the fuckers had drugged her!

That wasn't the only reason they were about to disappear tonight. It was one thing to be annoying and pushy with women. Drugging and an attempt to rape? That crossed a goddamned line.

He glanced at Wes and Bowie, who knocked out on the pavement. They'd need to be handled, but he couldn't exactly leave the woman alone.

A text later and both Hammer and Asher were by his side. They didn't need explanation. They could see the crime.

"Want me to take her to her room?" Hammer offered.

Amarok knew Hammer could be trusted. The man would never take advantage. But this was something Rok had to do himself.

"I've got her. You handle these assholes." Because while he might not be Alpha of an official pack, this was his town. His people. His responsibility. Even the visitors.

Gently, he scooped her into his arms and then eyed the lodge. He couldn't exactly walk through the front door. That would cause too many questions and probably end with the cops showing up. No way would they believe him innocent—at least until she woke up. Spending the night in a cell wasn't his idea of a good time.

Best he use the rear entrance, which was locked, but a quick search of her jacket pocket found her keycard.

Beep. He was inside with no idea what floor she was on or what room. Fuck. It meant sticking his head through every stairwell door and giving the hallway a sniff until he found the right one. He followed his nose to her room and let himself in.

Using the heel of his foot, he closed the door and then headed for the bed to dump her.

She barely stirred, murmuring in her drugged slumber. She'd have to sleep it off. He turned to leave, only to catch sight of her shoes and jacket.

She'd be fine.

You wouldn't leave one of your friends like this. This was just like the times he'd taken care of Lochlan, the oldest guy on the ranch at over forty and a man haunted by his past.

Her shoes were easy to slide off, but the coat required handling her body, tugging her arms free, and then removing it. The rest of her clothes—bra, jeans—would have to stay. He didn't want her waking and panicking. Wondering what might have happened.

Nothing happened because he'd been just in time to rescue her. A few minutes more? It didn't bear thinking.

My hero.

If she only knew. He was far from a hero even if he wasn't a villain. Rok had become a man who didn't tolerate bullshit. Just look at how he'd handled Wes and Bowie. It should be noted his guys wouldn't kill them in cold blood, but they would dump their rapist asses deep in the woods. Naked with only their wits, of which, between the pair, they didn't have many. They could technically survive and find their way out. Unless something hungry found them first.

Like a wolf.

He eyed the lady in the bed, sleeping peacefully. Her delicate features were a reminder she didn't belong here. Judging by the items packed by the door, she planned to return home.

He should, too, but he remained rooted to the floor. Once he walked out that door, he'd never see her again. Guided by an impulse he didn't understand, he returned to the side of the bed. What if she woke groggy? Afraid? What if she reacted badly and puked? People had died from choking on their own vomit.

Fuck.

Since the room only had one bed, and the chair looked uncomfortable as all hell, he sat on the floor, back to the door. He pulled out his phone and sent another text.

Gonna stick around and make sure the drug passes thru.

He got a thumbs-up in reply. He should sleep but instead found himself remembering the website she'd written down. It loaded, and the first thing he saw was a banner of her and the beaver, cheek to cheek, both with their teeth out in a grin.

Nope. He wasn't doing this. He shoved the phone in his pocket, closed his eyes, willed himself to sleep. Hadn't quite managed it when she stirred and mumbled, "I don't feel good."

In seconds, he was by her side. He carried her to the bathroom then held her hair while she puked. When she finished, he wiped her mouth and face with a warm cloth and handed her a glass of water.

"Rinse and spit," he ordered.

She'd yet to say anything but did as told, swirling and spitting a few times before grabbing her toothbrush for a scrub. Which was when he left her alone in the bathroom. She emerged a few minutes later. Wan. A bit shaky.

"Get back to bed." He sprang to guide her as her first trembling step had her swaying. She crawled under the covers and closed her eyes the moment her head hit the pillow.

He thought she went right back to sleep, only to hear her say, "Thank you."

For some reason it angered him. Not the thanks but the fact she'd even needed him to protect her. What kind of world let people abuse those weaker than them?

The same kind that let an alpha beat on his son for the simple fact he existed.

A few hours later, one more puking incident, and the worst of the drug having passed through her, he deemed it safe to leave.

He had to. The rage inside was building. Hard. Intense.

Only one thing would assuage it.

His howl could be heard for kilometers around.

The white wolf, a legend in these parts, was on the hunt.

SIX

A PASTY MOUTH GREETED MEADOW IN THE morning, but it could have been worse. She had no problem remembering those pushy men from the night before. The way they'd drugged her, intending nefarious deeds.

Then rescue by the most handsome man she'd ever met.

A glance showed her room empty. Mr. Fleetfoot was gone, but she remembered he'd stayed long enough to ensure she was okay. Held her hair as she puked. No wonder he'd fled.

She grimaced as she peeled her jeans and bra off, the marks left overnight in her skin painful to the touch. The shower was welcome, and a brush of her teeth got rid of the sour taste left behind. Her head was still a bit cloudy, but coffee and food would probably fix that right up. She had time before checkout.

She decided to brave the restaurant with its macabre display rather than leave the lodge. Emerging on the main floor it was to see it mostly deserted but for one man.

A smile spread across her face. "Mr. Fleetfoot!"

He appeared startled even as he approached her. "My name's Amarok. Rok to my friends."

Rok. She liked it. Strong. Dependable. Just like him. "And I'm Meadow. Meadow Fields." Which always caused people to groan. Her parents thought it amusing though. "What a delight to see you. Thank you for your assistance last night."

His expression darkened. "Don't thank me for doing the right thing."

"You went above and beyond." Only her mother ever stayed by her side when she had an upset tummy.

"Bah." He scowled. The type of man who didn't like compliments.

"What brings you here this morning?"

He grimaced. "You."

One word and it warmed her head to toe. "Aren't you just the cutest, checking in on me. As you can see, I'm fine, thanks to you! Although I am hungry. Are you hungry?" she babbled, and yet she couldn't stop herself. There was just something about this man...

"Yeah. I guess I could eat." He ran a hand through his hair as he glanced at the podium in front of the restaurant. "Don't suppose we could go somewhere else?"

"Please! That place is creepy." She almost begged.

A hint of a smile tugged his lips. "Come on. I know a place."

He led her outside but, rather than walk, headed for a beast of a truck. So big she eyed the daunting height to the passenger seat.

Standing behind her, he chuckled. "Need a boost?"

"If it's not a bother."

Right away, his hands spanned her waist and he lifted. There was nothing inappropriate at all in his touch, and yet she sucked in a breath and tingled.

He slammed the truck door and climbed into the seat beside her. He smelled of the woods. Fresh and crisp.

The truck started with a mighty rumble. "Goodness, it's loud."

"Because it runs on horsepower, not hamster." He said it so deadpan it took a moment to realize he joked.

She laughed. "Don't dismiss my Ladybug. She might be tiny and quiet, but she's dependable and, best of all, friendly to the planet."

He snorted. "Until a snowstorm hits and they don't find you until spring."

"I take transit or work from home on those days."

"Not an option out here," he noted as he drove a few minutes to a restaurant that was attached to a home. Mama's Grits read the hand-painted sign.

The inside was mismatched furniture, most of it worn out and wobbly on the sloping floor. The food was delicious and copious. She couldn't finish hers, but Amarok did. The man could eat, but he didn't speak much, meaning she spent most of the breakfast hogging the conversation, telling him all about nothing. Seriously. He must think her so boring, and yet he spent the meal staring at her.

When she tried to pay, he growled. Like literally growled, "I got this."

Then they got back in his truck. The thrill of him lifting her remained just as intense. It was only as they pulled into the lodge, he finally said, "So I've been thinking."

"Yes?" She glanced at him, and his gaze met hers.

"I—" He shook his head and looked away before saying, "I was thinking that if you're really that keen on studying the beaver, you can. But only for a week."

"Really!" She squealed, clapped, and bounced in her seat.

"Yeah, really, but with some rules, though, to keep you safe."

"Anything you say."

"Don't be so quick to agree."

"I'd do anything for my beaver."

"Jeezus," he hissed.

"Are you religious?"

"No. But I am apparently insane."

"More like wonderful." In her excitement she threw herself across the middle console and hugged him. No surprise, he stiffened. She continued to squeeze him nonetheless. When she pulled back, she chirped, "How soon can I start playing with my beaver?"

He coughed and turned away. "Today, I guess."

"Yay. I'll pack my things and head over. Thank you." On impulse, she leaned in and gave him a quick peck on the cheek and whispered, "You're the best. My beaver and I thank you." Then she hopped out of his truck and ran to the lodge before he could change his mind.

SEVEN

As if it wasn't bad enough what he pictured each time she said the word beaver, she'd she kissed him! Why the fuck did she have to go and do that?

The touch of her lips on his flesh burned him all the way home. A long ride because he not only gave her permission to study one fucking beaver, he'd also waited for her to pack that ridiculous, tiny car of hers —impressively he might add. He'd been convinced it wouldn't all fit and when it did, that it would prob- ably tilt over. But she got it putting along the road, and Rok followed it.

No surprise, she drove the speed limit. Probably sang along to the radio, too. She certainly did talk a lot. Usually that would drive him nuts, but she was so animated about everything. Being a man, he couldn't help but wonder if she'd be that excitable in bed.

Bet I could pleasure her hard enough she runs out of breath.

The very idea made him fucking hard. What was it about her that attracted him? Fascinated him to the point he said yes to her request? He never said yes. She'd pegged him correctly as a "no" kind of man and didn't seem daunted. The woman had no fear of him.

Like no fear at all.

She thought him a hero. A good guy. One she could just hug and kiss as if it were nothing. It set off a baffling chain reaction within that now had him craving her even more than ever.

Perhaps he should just fuck her and get it over with. Sink between her thighs until she clamped hard around his cock as she came.

He shuddered like an inexperienced boy with no control at the thought. Then found himself suddenly terrified. What if once wasn't enough? What if—

He pinched his lips. He wouldn't think it because he didn't believe in it.

Meadow eventually pulled into his driveway without losing her car to the wildlife. He'd worried about a Sasquatch deciding it wanted a shiny Hot Wheels car. According to his uncle, it had happened once before. The driver escaped. The car didn't survive being vroomed and shoved down a steep hill.

Despite no one being outside, their arrival didn't go unnoticed. A text pinged.

Wassup? Why is hamster lady back?

How to explain he'd changed his mind? She should have been driving back to the city at this very moment. She'd been ready to go. Then he opened his mouth. Now she'd be underfoot for the next week. Staying in his house because he sure as fuck couldn't let her sleep outside.

Maybe he should go camping during that time. *And leave her alone with the boys and Nova?* Jealousy reared hot and fierce. It made no sense.

He held it back as he texted. *Meadow is gonna check on the beaver. Make sure everyone knows to steer clear of that area.*

Meadow, eh? There was a string of emojis mocking Rok after that.

His jaw tightened, and he hesitated to reply because his attention got snagged as Meadow emerged from her car for a stretch. The lift of her arms pulled her shirt high enough he got a peek of skin. A lickable strip.

He was being a perv while Asher waited for a reply.

He typed, *Felt bad about her trouble in town.*

Thought I'd make it up to her. He hit Send too quick and regretted it immediately.

Especially since Asher didn't give the expected reply. He should have mocked Rok's softness.

Instead, *Path by the woodshed is clear, but she shouldn't go alone the first time.*

Asher was right. While only a twenty-minute walk, it put her far from help if she ran into something too stupid to recognize wolf territory.

Asher texted again. *Want me to take her?*

No. I'll do it. He typed it so fast he blinked.

Aren't you supposed to be doing paperwork? Asher reminded.

Reece, the guy who kept everything running smoothly, insisted on them going over the most boring details.

It can wait. I'll take her.

The only answer that eased his irrational jealousy, which he wasn't going to question right now. Must be the approaching full moon making him feel off.

He hopped out of the truck, a thump of two booted feet. The laces were undone, so he could easily kick them off.

Meadow reached into her car and into the pile filling it. In an impressive Jenga move, she pulled out a sweater and a hat.

"You got bug spray?" he asked, joining her, thumbs tucked in his belt loops.

"Yes." She nodded. "Although I don't usually get eaten."

Then she'd not met the right wolf.

Bad. Mind out of the gutter.

She reached in, bending over in a way that had him quickly shifting his gaze from her ass, because that would really lead to some X-rated thoughts.

She emerged with a bag and dangled it. "I also have the stuff to rub on if I do get a bite."

He'd help her rub, although everyone knew saliva would do the trick in a pinch. He'd lick every inch of her.

There went his thoughts again.

He glanced to the woods. "There's a path from here to the creek. It's about a twenty-minute walk."

"Fantastic. Is it okay if I use your bathroom first? I'm not big on the peeing in the woods and carrying around my tissue in a bag." Her nose wrinkled.

His did, too. Men had it much easier when it came to pissing. "Of course, you can use it. Bathroom's right off the front door, and there's another by the kitchen mudroom entrance."

"Yay!" She skipped off to use it, and he stared at her ass. No man could have resisted that sweet bouncing thing.

His phone pinged. No words just a drooling emoji.

He lifted a middle finger. No privacy.

By the time Meadow emerged, he'd had a chance to regret his invitation and practice a speech to revoke it.

A speech that died as she approached grinning. "That is some wallpaper you got in there." She spoke of the newspaper clippings that dated back decades, snipped out and then glued to the wall. It made for interesting reading while on the can.

"So listen, about the beaver—"

"I can guess what you'll say given it's obvious you're an animal man. I won't disturb Weaver. Promise. I know better than to muck around habitats or sully their hunting grounds. I will stay out of the way. Scout's honor." She crossed her heart.

Telling her no now was the equivalent of kicking a pup being cute. He sighed. "Don't litter."

"That goes without asking."

"Don't wander off from that area."

"I'll stick to the path, no worries."

Would she stop being so fucking amenable?

Before he could say something to finally wipe her smile, an ATV came whipping around the side of the house, driven by Darian, bareheaded and looking grim, which wasn't unusual. Most of those at the ranch were grumpy fuckers with the exception of Asher, who could be his nastiest when he smiled.

Darian pulled up and offered a nod to Meadow. The engine turned off, and he swung a leg saying, "You must be the beaver hunter I've heard all about."

"Not a hunter! Goodness. I could never kill anything. I shoot videos and study so I can share a comprehensive learning experience with those who love those beautiful and majestic beavers like I do."

For some reason, neither he nor Darian laughed despite it being the most ridiculous thing ever. How could they when SHE MEANT EVERY SINGLE FUCKING WORD?

She was nuts and so fucking cute it hurt even more.

Darian remained sober. "He's an interesting fellow. I can see why you'd want to study him. Did you perhaps want company? Someone who knows the land?"

Wait, was Darian flirting with his Meadow?

Rok glowered. "I'll be sticking close to her to make sure she doesn't run into trouble."

"Someone else should do that because you have things to do."

"I'll handle the paperwork later," he grumbled.

"Not later. Your attention is required now."

Darian gave him a pointed look that said this was more than regular business.

"She can't go alone." Darian opened his mouth, but before he could offer his services again, Rok wheeled and jabbed a finger in Lochlan's direction as he emerged from the workshop. "Loch, you will escort Meadow."

Lochlan's epic dark scowl managed to double. "Fuck off. I ain't a babysitter."

"Oh, you don't need to bother anyone for me. I am quite comfortable in the woods," Meadow interjected.

"If you mention that bell..." he threatened.

"I have it. And I practiced ringing it really hard." She smiled impishly.

Was she fucking joking? Darian's chuckle indicated she just had.

"Lucky for you, no bears in that section. But you don't want to stray far from that area. Once you're out of sight of that creek, and the path, it's really easy to get turned around," Darian said.

"You're sending her to the new beaver dam?" Lochlan suddenly veered toward them.

"Something wrong?" he asked.

"Current's still running fast since the storm two days ago."

"I wasn't planning on going in the water," Meadow replied.

"Still dangerous. Fuck." Lochlan grunted. "Lucky for you, I'm in the mood for fish. I'll drop a line and keep an eye while she plays explorer. Let's go."

"Thank you!" She clapped her hands. "I just need to grab a few things."

While Lochlan rolled his eyes, she popped her trunk.

It physically hurt Rok to see the lack of space. Whereas Darian breathed, "How the fuck did she pull it out without dumping it all on the ground?"

Because she was nuts. And so was he. "Later." He walked off with Darian. *Don't look back.*

Hard to do when she chirped, "Thank you again, Rocky. You are the best!"

He winced, not sure which was worse. The compliment or the fucking name.

Darian outright snickered. "Rocky? Someone made an impression. What happened? I take it this has to do with Wes and Bowie getting dumped past the ravine? Asher and Hammer told me about it when they got home."

On four feet since they decided to leave Rok the truck in town.

"They assaulted and drugged her." No more needed to be said.

Darian went quiet before saying, "So that's why you didn't come home last night."

"She was pretty out of it. Just wanted to make sure she'd be okay."

"And then took her to breakfast."

He winced. Someone had seen and reported. Fucking small towns. It was a wonder he and the crew at the ranch managed to keep any secrets. "She was hungry."

"Why not just admit you like her?"

Like seemed tame for the inferno that swept him when she was around. "She's cute."

Darian snickered. "Which is why you sent her off with Lochlan. The man hates cute."

Did he? Because he'd ended up going of his own volition. Volunteering even. What was that about? Surely Lochlan had no interest in Meadow. He never paid women any attention.

But Meadow was different...

"Are you listening?"

"What?"

"Get your head out of your pants for a minute. I gotta show you something."

"You going to tell me what, or is it a surprise?" he muttered with only a hint of sarcasm.

"Remember how the other day someone pissed on the raspberries and didn't leave a trace?"

"Yeah. Did we find more piss?"

"Not quite."

They were well behind the house, heading for the gardens maintained by those with a green thumb, meaning Astra and Gary.

"Poppy sent me out for some veggies for dinner. That's how I found the footprint."

No need to ask. It wasn't one of theirs. "What can you tell me about it?"

"Look for yourself."

Darian indicated one of the well-tended boxed beds. The dark soil moist, leafy green tops bushy by the row. Set very clearly in the dirt was a five-toed footprint.

"No shoes?" Rok crouched but getting closer didn't net a scent.

"That's not the only thing. I just found the one footprint."

"Impossible." He glanced around. "There must be something else."

"I looked." Given Darian was no slouch at tracking, that said something.

"There has to be something. Everyone leaves a trace." Footprints might be easy to hide but scent, presence, had a tendency to linger.

"Nada, hence, the mystery."

Rok ran his fingers over the ground. There was crushed stone between the raised beds. Someone walking wouldn't leave a print.

He made his way to the edge closest to the woods and kept looking. He came across all kinds of normal scents: rabbit, squirrel, chipmunk, raccoon, fox.

No pungent, earthy aroma of bear. Nothing human. Just the scents of those he lived with.

The footprint was a mystery. One he didn't like because it could only mean one thing. "Someone is fucking with us."

EIGHT

MEADOW HUMMED AS SHE SET UP A SPACE FOR herself in full sight of the dam Weaver had built. Weatherproof cushion to sit on. Book. Snack because breakfast was a while ago and a tripod holding her camera, which was set on detect motion.

She'd not seen Weaver yet, but she could tell by her tracking device he was nearby. Would he remember her?

She'd certainly been permanently marked by her experience with him. His mother had come to the sanctuary injured and pregnant. She didn't survive, but her baby did. Meadow had spent countless nights with Weaver, cradling him close to keep him snuggly warm, feeding him milk via a dropper. But she'd been responsible enough that once he could start eating on his own, she put him outside to run around in their treed acreage. The sanctuary even had a pond, which he tried to build a dam in with the saplings he felled.

Then the storm hit, flattening part of the fence and flooding their yard, including the building that housed the animals. To save them, they'd had to release them. Not all of them were recovered. Weaver was found, but because he'd managed to survive for months on his own, animal activists protested for his right to be free.

And won.

The tracking device was Meadow's desperate last-ditch idea to see if that proved to be the right decision, arguing they should know for future cases. Thus far, it seemed as if Weaver's freedom worked. He'd travelled far from home. Built himself a lovely dam on a creek. Best of all, he remained alive.

As part of her documenting, she took pictures and measurements, got all that without incident. It was when she rinsed her hand from her sticky apple that she managed to fall in the water, which crisp and caused her to gasp. She emerged, soaking wet, to find Rok standing on the bank.

"Rocky!"

"What the fuck?"

She beamed. "Just refreshing myself."

"I thought you were told no playing in the water."

"Apparently nature thought I need a bath. Good thing I keep my phone in a waterproof case." She held it up.

He arched a brow. "You don't appear to be as protected."

"I'm a little wet." She shrugged off her damp jacket to find her shirt underneath soaked through, the fabric clinging to her skin, especially her breasts.

He noticed, even stared for a second with smoldering eyes before he turned away. "Do you have dry things to change into?"

"In the car."

"Let's go then. It's time for dinner anyhow."

"Really? You don't have to feed me. I did bring some stuff," she stated, shivering a bit as the wet fabric attracted the late afternoon breeze.

"I highly doubt it will be as good as what Poppy makes. Lochlan caught a few fish for dinner."

"He's quite impressive. I swear the fish jumped onto that man's hook on purpose."

"It helps they're plentiful," was his grumbled reply. "Anyone can fish like a champ in that creek."

"I can see why you love living here. It's so beautiful." She spun as they followed the path going past her minicamp. Her knapsack hung in a tree to keep it away from ants and most pests. She hung her coat beside it. "It should be dry by morning."

"There's no food in the bag?" he asked.

"I know better." She laughed. Her bathroom breaks were when she grabbed a snack from her car. Although, on her second trip in to use the bathroom, the Poppy he'd mentioned made her take a banana muffin and an iced tea. Delicious.

"Did you get a lot of good images?" he asked, head down, hands shoved in his pockets. Stiff, as if small talk didn't come easily.

"Tons of pics, but not of Weaver. But that's par for the course with him. Even as a little guy he was a night beaver. I'm hoping he comes out tonight. The moon is almost full, and the sky is supposed to be clear, meaning I should be able to spot him easily."

"You want us to come back out tonight?"

"You don't have to. Now that I know where I'm going, I'll be perfectly fine."

"Says the woman who fell in the creek after being told to stand clear."

"I won't be anywhere close to the water at night."

"No, you won't because you won't be out here. Too dangerous."

Overprotective, how adorable. "Don't worry, Rocky. I've done this before."

"Not in these woods you haven't," was his dark

reply. "And it's Rok, not Rocky." He took the term brooding to new heights.

"Then I guess you'll have to be my hero again and keep me safe." The flirtatious words left her mouth, and he immediately stumbled.

"Fucking tree roots." The path was smooth.

She inwardly smiled and then kept grinning at dinner. Apparently, while Rok might own the ranch, he wasn't some snobby guy who kept apart from his workers. They not only lived in the house and the various cabins scattered nearby, but they also ate together at the massive table—two tables pushed together actually—with benches on either side. It made for a large gathering and lots of listening as she tried to grasp who was who.

There was Darian, a serious guy, brother to Poppy. She was also somber but in a more tragic sense. Her cooking, though, had to be most joyful thing Meadow had ever put in her mouth.

Asher appeared to be the playful one of the group, teasing and chuckling constantly, in direct contrast to the very grouchy Lochlan, who rarely said much or cracked a smile. Although he'd been the one to tell her that Weaver chose a fine spot for his dam.

Reece, who apparently handled the ranch books, sat by his husband, Gary, whose tomatoes were doing very well this year. Although, according to

Astra, who was very pregnant and married to Bellamy, her crop of eggplants, while of lesser volume, was impressive due to it being more difficult.

Nova was the last woman in the group. Her hair was undercut so it shagged on top, and her eyes were a vivid blue. Her nose piercing sported a jewel that matched them.

Missing were Hammer and Wallace.

A lot of people who might not be related but laughed and talked like family.

Meadow drank it in and soon was conversing just as animatedly as the others. Rok didn't say much, but she found him eyeing her often.

Around eight, she stood and said, "I should get out there and grab those pictures."

"I'll come with you," Rok volunteered and rose to his feet immediately, which led to some quieting and many eyes suddenly trained on him. "I'll be back later," he gruffly added, moving stiffly as if embarrassed.

Such a funny man, and she'd get to spend time alone with him. Under a glowing moon.

Anything could happen.

She first used the bathroom before joining him outside. He stared up at the sky. She headed for her car and the things she'd need.

He eyed her bundle and frowned. "Sleeping bag?"

"To stay warm, of course. A little chilly at night to be sleeping without a blanket."

"What? You're not sleeping outside. I'll find you a spot in the house."

"I don't want to put anyone out. It's okay. I do this all the time."

Before he could reply, she jammed her headband on and lit the lamp.

He hissed. "What the fuck are you doing now?"

"Light to see in the dark, silly. Not all of us know the path that well."

"I wouldn't have let you fall." He sounded most put out.

"I'm starting to think you like saving me," she teased as she skipped for the woods, only to find herself halted.

"Give me that." He insisted on carrying everything. Just like Lochlan with her knapsack. Chivalry was not dead.

As they strolled through the woods, she breathed deep. "You're so lucky to live here."

"It is a nice place."

"It's beyond nice. It's perfection. I could stay here forever."

"But aren't. We agreed on a week," he stressed.

She laughed. "I won't overstay my welcome. Promise. Just envious you get to wake up to paradise every day."

"If you like it so much, why live in the city?" The question showed he'd been paying attention at dinner as she spoke with the others.

"It has everything close by. Friends. Family. My job." She grimaced.

"Sounds like that last bit isn't all that great."

"It is. Was. We're having problems lately because animal activists think we should shut down."

"My understanding from what I heard at dinner is your sanctuary helps critters abandoned or injured."

"We do, and they're okay with that. But they think the moment we fix them we should toss them back in the wild." Glancing ahead to where she could hear the creek, she added, "I used to think they were wrong. But if Weaver, who was born in captivity can make it, then could be they're right."

"Not necessarily. It's a two-edged answer. On the one hand, there is something to be said for freedom. To be able to roam and do whatever they want. But on the other, it's dangerous in the wild. There is more to it than just securing food and shelter but staying safe from predators and the weather."

"So how do we know the right answer?"

"We don't. But I will say as someone who deals with animals in captivity, the biggest difference is in how you treat them. Treat them right and it's not a prison."

An answer she approved of. "My research shows the ranch raises a few types of animals. Alpacas, bison, and sheep. Weird mix."

He shrugged. "The last two are just continuing what my uncle started."

"Reece says he was the one who talked you into the alpacas."

"Yeah. They're the real moneymakers these days."

"And so cute!" Always smiling for the camera. She grinned at him and found him watching her.

His amber eyes flashed as her headlight caught them, and for a moment, he reminded her of a wild animal.

"I'm blind!" he complained.

"Sorry. Guess I should go into stealth mode now that we're nearby." She turned off the light and spent a moment blinking to adjust.

"Stay close so you don't fall in the water again," he grumbled.

She did as told, sticking to his heels, meaning when he stopped, she smacked into him and bounced. Landed on her ass with an oomph.

He turned around and cast a moonlit shadow. "Seriously! Are you okay?"

"Yup. Just clumsy." She held out a hand, and he hauled her up. But rather than let go, he drew her close.

She tilted her chin to look at him. His intent stare had her licking her lips.

"Be careful." He stepped away.

He didn't come near her at all for the next hour as she took pictures, finally seeing Weaver in the flesh as he swam out of his dam. He'd gotten even bigger since she last saw him.

She cried tears of joy when she murmured, "Weavie, baby," and he changed direction swimming for her. He crawled from the water into her lap and let her pet him as she crooned happily.

When he finally swam off, she turned damp eyes on Rok. "He remembered me!"

"I'd say you have that effect on everyone you meet."

A compliment that had her blushing.

As she predicted, the beaver was set for a busy night of gnawing. She unrolled her sleeping bag in a spot she could watch. Rok melted into the shadows, and she assumed he kept watch. Or despite all his grumbling about danger, he could have left.

She doubted that, though. The man had strong protective instincts.

When he did finally appear, it was behind her to whisper, "It's late. Time for bed."

She craned to see him. "I'm sorry. I should have told you to leave a while ago since I'm spending the night here."

"Like fuck you are."

NINE

"You can't camp outside." On this, he wouldn't budge.

"Why not?"

"Because a sleeping bag isn't enough."

"I assure you, it's warm enough for this time of year, and it has face netting for bugs."

"Won't stop a real predator. Like a wolf."

She scoffed. "Wolves rarely bother people unless they're starving. It's late summer. They won't be desperate yet."

"There are bears."

"Also fat from a plentiful summer. Besides, I have my—"

"Don't you dare say it."

"Bell." She said it. And then doubled down. "Plus, I brought some cayenne pepper."

As she listed the dumbest things he'd ever heard, he realized there was only one way to shut her up.

He mashed his mouth to hers.

She gasped but didn't push him away. Her lips softened and parted against his. Her hands reached and clung to his neck. A groan escaped him, almost a growl as need filled him. Pulsed inside.

He wanted her. Here. Now.

Madness. He tore his mouth free. "Sorry." It emerged gruff.

"Why? I've been hoping all day you'd kiss me."

And then it was her turn to grab him and drag him down to press her lips to his. Kissing him, making little happy sounds that drove him wild.

She ended up lying down on her sleeping bag, him half atop her, his mouth unable to get enough of her. Her writhing didn't deter his hands from their exploration. He tucked them under her shirt to stroke over smooth skin. Brushed rounded curves contained by a bra. A hand between her legs had her arching, the heated core of her scorching even with her pants.

He rubbed, sucking at her tongue as he stroked her, torturing them both by keeping their clothes on.

She keened against his lips, and he fumbled with her zipper like he'd not done since his first time. He slipped his hand past her panties and pants to find the core of her. Wet and wanting.

Her sex sucked the finger he inserted. She panted into his mouth and rocked in time to his finger-fucking thrusts.

She came with a shudder that had him growling and nipping at her bottom lip. He would have taken her, right then and there, if not for the howl.

A howl that didn't belong.

TEN

Meadow floated on a cloud of bliss, her body sated and yet still throbbing. She wanted more of his touch.

Him inside her.

It took a second to realize Rok had hauled her to her feet, but not for more fun times. He'd returned to his usual grumpy self. "We have to go."

"Go where?"

"Back to the house."

Given the passion they'd indulged in a moment ago, she assumed it was to have sex. A bed would be nice. "Let me put this away." Nothing worse than coming back to some critters having taken over her stuff.

"Leave it," he growled.

The caveman routine? Totally sexy. "Okay, but if

a skunk makes my sleeping bag its new home, you're the one washing it."

He didn't reply, rather grabbed her hand and dragged her along. Eager. So eager. She'd never had a man rush her to bed. She'd never had a man make her come outside either. Usually, those kinds of passionate things only happened in books.

They made it to his house. Many lights in the various rooms were lit, as were some of the little cabins. Only then did he slow down, his head turning left and right.

Alert. For what? Had he heard something in the woods? She certainly hadn't unless her own huffing breath counted.

"Is something wrong?"

"You need to get inside." That didn't sound like a lover's invitation. He swung open the door and waited for her to enter.

Given his stony expression, she debated going inside. What did she really know of this man? Val always said she was too trusting.

"Close the door. You're letting in a draft," Astra complained from the living room. "Baby doesn't like the cold."

"Then winter's going to suck," was Nova's reply.

Meadow entered, and he followed, stepping past her to the living room. It was a cozy space with a massive couch holding Astra and Bellamy and a plush club chair, which held Nova. Another couch sat across from her.

The television stretched over the top of the currently unlit fireplace. Astra wore a blanket while Bellamy wore shorts and a T-shirt. According to Astra, who'd chatted with Meadow at dinner, it used to be she ran hot, until pregnancy messed with her hormones.

Nova set aside her phone to ask, "Did you see your beaver?"

"We did. It was amazing," Meadow enthused.

"I'll bet it was," Nova drawled.

Amarok growled. "Not right now, Nova. We might have a wolf situation. I'm going to check it out but wanted to drop off Meadow first. Can you take care of her?

"Fuck babysitting your girlfriend. I'm going with you."

"I'll settle Meadow for the night," Astra offered, holding out her hand, which was a signal for Bellamy to rise and heave. He exaggerated with a groan and received a jab in the stomach as reply. It made him laugh.

"Don't laugh," scowled his wife. "Because you're going with them."

"But I was just about to have popcorn with butter. You know you want some..." He cajoled.

"I do, but you know I like it better the morning after, so make it when you get back." She kissed his cheek.

Amarok turned to leave. So much for having sex tonight. Apparently, Amarok took his ranching serious.

They left, and Astra closed the door and locked it. She smiled. "They'll be gone at least an hour or more. Would you like a snack?"

"I would."

Astra made lots of fresh popcorn so she could have some left over. They watched a baby show that had Astra groaning as if in pain. "Shit should not go up to their ears."

They chatted, Astra asking her about her life in the city. Her family. Then Astra shared anecdotes of her own family but was quite frank about their estrangement. "It was my family or Bellamy. I chose him."

Meadow had to wonder if she could walk away from hers. Then again, they'd never not supported her. Whatever decision she made in love or life, they'd be by her side.

"You seem very happy," Meadow ventured.

Astra nodded. "Never realized how shitty my life

was until I got away from it. You ever wonder what it would be like elsewhere?"

The question deserved a truthful answer. "My life isn't horrible. But..." She bit her lip. "It is boring. Predictable. Which sounds so privileged."

"You're allowed to want things," was Astra's sage advice. "It's okay to fantasize about something more. I pursued my fantasy, and now I have my baby to look forward to." She put a hand on her distended stomach.

"Because you found the thing that makes you happy. I'm still looking."

"Are you sure you didn't just find it?" Astra teased. "I saw how you looked when you and Rok got here. Like a woman kissed."

Despite not being a virgin, Meadow blushed. "That obvious?"

"Very. Rok likes you." Stated as if it were a fact.

"You think? Because it's hard to tell," Meadow admitted. "He scowls a lot."

"Yeah, he does, but I'll tell you one thing. If he didn't like you, you wouldn't be here. He's picky about who he lets on the ranch."

"Have you been here long?"

Astra nodded. "Going on five years now. He invited us to live here and didn't care about the fact me and Bellamy aren't exactly the ideal couple."

She frowned. "You seem perfect for each other."

Astra smiled. "We think so, too, but our families respectively decided they hated each other. They forbade us."

"That's horrible. But kind of romantic? Like Romeo and Juliet."

Astra laughed. "I guess, except we didn't die. Honestly, their ultimatum was the best thing that could have happened to us. It got us out of the cesspool cities we lived in, and now we get to enjoy paradise every day."

"It is lovely here." Meadow sighed. "A part of me hates I have to leave in a week."

"Maybe you won't have to. You and Rok appear to have hit it off."

"Have we?" Because she had to wonder given the way he'd run off first chance he got.

"Rok's never brought a girl home before."

"Technically, he didn't bring me here. He simply agreed to let me study Weaver for a week."

"After saying no. He never changes his mind."

Apparently, he had changed his mind about Meadow, because he'd rather go dally with a wolf than play with her. "Even if he did like me, dating would be impossible. We don't exactly live close."

"You said it was beautiful. That you'd love to live here."

"I would enjoy it; however, isn't it kind of stalk-erish to suddenly decide to move towns because of a guy?" Her nose wrinkled. Her spontaneity only went so far.

"Not just any guy. *The* guy." Astra didn't hide the fact she believed in romance.

"But where would I work? Live?"

"Here."

Tempting but, at the same time, awkward. She barely knew Rok. She shook her head. "A week isn't long enough to move in with someone."

"Bellamy and I met at college and were sharing a dorm room within three days." Proudly stated. "My roommate couldn't wait to switch. Claimed they couldn't sleep a wink." Astra giggled, and Meadow couldn't help but join in.

Then Astra paused and grabbed her belly. "Someone is kick-boxing in there. Whoa, baby. I can't wait to pop this puppy out. I swear I've never peed so much in my life. Do you want kids?"

"Loads of them. But we'll see. My mom had a hard time conceiving me. And I take after her."

"Rok loves kids. He says he doesn't want to be a dad, but he'd be a good one."

"Why doesn't he want any?"

"Let's just leave it at a crappy childhood."

Meadow had so many questions about him but

knew better than to pry. Some things should come from the man himself. "He seems to have done well for himself."

"He has. And he's not bad to look at."

Try ridiculously handsome. "He's sweet, too."

"Rok, sweet?" Astra started laughing.

"In a gruff way. That involves much scowling."

Astra snickered. "Betcha he wasn't grumbling when he was kissing you."

Her cheeks heated. "Can't have been that great. He heard a wolf, and he was hauling me back to the house double time."

"Wolves can be a serious thing out here. Better safe than sorry." Astra yawned. "Bedtime for me. Let's get you settled for the night."

By settled, Astra meant Rok's room, situated toward the back of the house.

"I shouldn't." She shook her head with unusual hesitation. It was one thing to be bold with him, but to assume he wanted her in his bed...

"Given the spare room lost its bed for a crib, this is the only option. Knowing Rok, he'd set the couch on fire before asking you to sleep on it."

"I really would be fine going back to my sleeping bag in the woods. I do this all the time." There was a lovely park outside the city she camped in. It wasn't quite this wild, though.

"Nope. Rok brought you here to keep you safe. This is safe." Astra motioned her into the huge space, the wide plank floor covered at random by rag woven rugs. The bed was king sized with two pillows and a plaid comforter. A fireplace in front was set with wood, ready to burn. The two dressers were mismatched, as were the nightstands.

A comfortable room. *His* room. She instantly loved it.

A large sliding glass door led to the rear yard and a patio with an Adirondack chair.

Astra moved to the windows and pulled the curtains shut. "Just in case the boys come back through the yard, this will give you privacy to change. Bathroom is through there." Astra pointed. "You can borrow a shirt of his to sleep in. Top drawer, and he's got pants just under those."

"I have an overnight bag in the car."

Astra shook her head. "If there's a wolf out there, better you stay inside."

Just how dangerous were the wolves in this area?

Rather than argue, Meadow said, "Thank you." The idea of wearing his shirt did tempt.

"You're welcome. If you need anything, holler. Bellamy and I have a room down the hall."

Good to know. It was one thing to yell her pleasure in the woods. Another for everyone to hear.

Perhaps Rok would return soon and continue what he started. She still trembled from his touch. Ached for more.

Once Astra left, she washed up and found a shirt of his that held his scent lying over a chair. She almost put it on. The fact she sniffed it had her setting it down quickly instead.

Why was she acting so weird? Please don't let her be turning into a Joe. That Netflix series about the stalker was riveting.

She didn't need to change. She already wore comfortable stuff for a night outside. She eyed the bed. It didn't feel right to sleep in here without his permission. She was all for being bold and going after what she wanted, but there had to be mutual consent. This was his space. She shouldn't invade it without his invitation.

The extra blanket and pillow on his bed were fair game, though. She returned with them to the empty living room. The couch was comfortable and wide, perfectly sized for her.

She snuggled under the blanket, cheek against a pillow that smelled of him. When she fell asleep, Rok featured in her dreams.

ELEVEN

"You're sure you heard howling?" Nova asked.

They'd found no traces of a wolf within a few miles of the ranch, making Rok wonder if he'd misheard. He'd sent Bellamy home while he checked around the barns again. Nova stuck with him.

"Could have sworn I did."

"I'm sure you had something howling. Maybe that woman you had with you?" Nova teased.

"Nothing happened," he growled.

"Says the man who forgot to wash the smell of pussy from his fingers," drawled Nova.

Apparently, Rok could still blush. "We fooled around. Big deal."

"It is a big deal since you've never brought a girl to the ranch before."

"I didn't bring her," he argued.

"Semantics. You personally invited her to spend a week. You couldn't wait to get down to the river with her after dinner. Can't really blame you. It's a nice night." Nova glanced up at the moon with its almost full girth.

"It wasn't like that." Only it was. He'd have fucked Meadow if not distracted by the howl.

"Sure, it wasn't. I'm thinking that howl was an excuse for you to run away."

"Run away from what?"

"Meadow. You like her."

"She's attractive."

"I think she's more than that. I saw you watching her."

"Was not." More lying. He couldn't help himself.

Nova snickered. "Whatever you say. Have fun. Don't wake the pregnant one." Nova veered for the garage, where she inhabited the loft. It was insulated and made cozy last year so she could have her own space.

Rok entered the house via the kitchen. He found Bellamy eating some popcorn.

"Astra will kill you if you don't leave some."

"I know. I'm gonna make more." Bellamy offered the buttery bowl. "Want some?"

"I'm good."

"Eager to find the woman." Bellamy nodded. "It was like that with me and Astra, too."

He blinked before exclaiming, "What the fuck are you yapping about?"

"You've met your mate."

"Have not," he sputtered.

"Dude, it's obvious. You don't have to look so horrified. Being mated ain't a bad thing," his friend said.

"Whoa. Who said anything about mating? She's hot. I want to bang her. Nothing more." Spoken almost defensively.

"If you say so."

"I do say so!"

"Then you'll miss out. Me, I thank the fates every morning when I wake up beside Astra that we found each other." Without a pack to shelter them, they chose to make their own way and found themselves at White Wolf Ranch.

His uncle never turned anyone away. He'd been collecting people even before Rok arrived after he left his dad's house.

"See you in the morning." Rok left the kitchen and wondered where Astra had stuck Meadow. Because he should avoid her.

Find her.

No. It was late. Waking her would be crazy.

He'd been crazy since the moment he met her. The scent of her clung to him. He couldn't escape it. Nor did he want to.

She'd been so responsive to his touch. Writhing and keening, eager for him. Wet. Sweet smelling.

I need her.

The primal urge moved his feet. Where was Meadow? Knowing Astra, she probably put Meadow in his room. Was she awake, waiting for him? Passionate and eager? Or disappointed he'd left her abruptly? Perhaps even mad?

Only one way to find out. He entered his bedroom quietly. The scent of her was all over it, teasing him.

Want her.

As he headed for the bed, he noticed it lacked a Meadow-sized lump. The top blanket remained pulled taut, but a pillow had gone missing and the extra covering at the foot was gone as well.

Where is she?

The scent of her drove him a little wild. It didn't explain the panic of not knowing where she was.

He returned to the main hall and followed his nose to the living room. He almost missed the tiny lump nestled under a blanket on the couch. She'd obviously eschewed his bed.

Meaning he had it to himself. Good. He could jack off in peace.

Or I could kiss her awake. Make her wet and ready for him that he might ease the ache in his balls. He'd have to take her to his bedroom lest Bellamy wander in.

He could fuck her in his bed. Make her cry out again as she came. But then what? He couldn't exactly kick her out after. He'd be stuck spending the night with her.

What if she wanted to cuddle?

It might lead to more sex.

Then there was the morning. What would he say? What would everyone think?

Knowing them, they'd assume the wrong thing.

She means fuck all. He was just feeling a bit over-sexed and needed a cold shower. And while he was at it, he should smack himself a few times for even thinking about molesting Meadow in her sleep.

He might live in the boonies, but he knew better than to take consent for granted. Just because she liked it before didn't mean she wanted it now.

No kissing unless she was awake and asking for it. Or, even better, no kissing at all. He had no room in his life for a human woman.

He went to leave, only to pause. Only a shitty host would leave her on a lumpy couch. He'd said she would spend the night inside. He would never ask Astra to give up her bed. The nursery obviously wouldn't suit. It left only one place to put her.

Meadow snuggled into his chest as he carried her to his bed. She sighed as she buried her face in his pillow. Left her scent all over his sheets.

How she tempted him to crawl in beside her.

He walked away and then had the crappiest fucking sleep on the couch. A couch not big enough to hold him.

The next day he opened his eyes to a brightly chirped, "Good morning!"

TWELVE

Meadow slept great but woke alone in Rok's bed. She had a vague recollection of him carrying her. He'd obviously not stayed. She found her chivalrous host in the living room, looking squished on the couch. What a gentleman.

She crouched beside him and resisted the urge to trace the lines of his face. What a beautiful man. His features were serene in repose.

His thick lashes fluttered, and when they opened, she couldn't help the joy filling her as she uttered an exuberant, "Good morning!"

Apparently, she'd startled him, because he rolled off the couch, flattening her under him.

Not a bad spot to be. She laughed. "Oops."

"Sorry. Fuck." Quickly he rolled off and rubbed a hand through his hair.

"Why did you sleep out here?" she asked.

"Because you're the guest. Couch was fine." He lied badly.

"Sharing the bed would have been better." She winked. "As a thank-you for letting me have it, let me make you breakfast."

"I should get going on my chores."

"In a minute. You need food first. You had a long night. Did you find the wolf?"

"No." He followed her to the kitchen, a towering presence that made her tingle with awareness. "Either I was mistaken, or it was farther out than expected."

They entered the kitchen to find Poppy flipping pancakes onto plates and bacon already stacked on another.

"Sit and I shall serve you," Meadow declared.

"You don't have to," he said.

"I insist. After all, you've been such a gentleman."

Poppy coughed. "I have a flan about to come out of the oven."

"Mmm. It's almost like my perfect dessert, but you can have it for breakfast." Meadow clapped her hands.

"What's the plan today?" Poppy asked as they sat at the massive kitchen counter with its stools. The living room might be tight, but the kitchen and attached dining area were huge.

"More Weaver watching."

"I can't take you," Rok declared in between mouthfuls. The man was so shy. Perhaps Astra wasn't exaggerating when she said he never brought women to meet his ranch family.

She also should remind herself she wasn't his woman.

Not yet.

"I can find it myself. It's not a difficult path."

"I'll go with her for a bit. I won't start prepping dinner until later since lunch is leftovers," Poppy offered.

"Stay out of the creek. It's still running harder than it looks."

"Yes, Daddy." Poppy rolled her eyes.

"Brat." Spoken gruffly but fondly. "I gotta go." He snared an apple and left with a quickly muttered, "See you later."

Was he talking to Meadow? In general?

Poppy grinned. "He is so smitten."

Another person who thought it. Meadow shook her head. "I'm not sure how you're getting that. He didn't even look at me as he left."

"Exactly." Poppy bobbed her head. "I hear you and Rok were making out last night."

Her cheeks heated. "Does everyone know?"

"Yup. This is Rok. He—"

"Doesn't bring girls he kisses here. I heard." She grimaced. "He doesn't seem too happy about it this morning."

"He's always grumpy in the morning. And afternoon. Evening I don't know. I'm usually working on my homework." Poppy was taking online college classes. "In his defense, he has lots to take care of."

"He seems very responsible."

"Because he is. Even before his uncle passed, he was taking care of everyone. Should have seen him when we had that problem with the bears."

"Bears?"

Poppy waved a hand. "Uh, yeah, but no worries. They don't come around anymore."

"Did he kill them?"

"No. More like scared them off. We should go. They say it might rain this afternoon."

Meadow visited her car to snare fresh clothes before having a shower. She put her dirty set with some items Poppy was loading in the machine.

They set out for the beaver dam. Chatting. Poppy was a sweet girl, if jumpy every time she heard something in the woods.

"I thought you said there are no bears?" Meadow teased the third time Poppy whirled.

She shrugged. "Old habit. I used to have a relative who liked to sneak up on me."

"They obviously traumatized you." Meadow frowned. "Not cool."

"When Darian found out, he took me out of there."

"Where were your parents when it was happening?"

"Dead. They died while my brother served in the military. The person watching over me wasn't nice." No need to say more. Meadow grasped the undertone.

"I'm glad you escaped." Meadow wondered if they all had a tragic story. Surely Asher with his easy smiles was the exception? Lochlan looked like he'd been born mad.

"Some days I worry I'll end up back there and that Darian won't be able to rescue me."

"Then you would rescue yourself." She squeezed the woman's hand. "Never let anyone mistreat you. Walk away. Find help. There are groups to shelter women around the country."

"Not from them," she muttered ominously. "But let's stop talking about me. What about you? Astra says you're thinking of staying past the week."

"What? No." They bantered back and forth.

Poppy, like Astra, was convinced Rok had it bad for Meadow. Meadow didn't quite see it.

He appeared angry around her, yes. Overly protective, too. But this morning he'd barely looked at her, let alone touched her.

Their arrival at Weaver's dam changed the tone of the conversation as Poppy took an interest in the mammal currently swimming back with his newest branch.

Eventually, though, Poppy wandered away, looking for mushrooms and other wild things to use in her kitchen while Meadow moved downstream, taking pictures. Soothed by the greenery and babble of water.

The flash of red proved unexpected. She paused and held her breath as she stared across the creek at an unexpected surprise. She quickly clicked a few shots before the creature ran off. She returned to Poppy flushed with excitement. "You'll never believe what I saw. The hugest fox."

"I doubt he was that big," Poppy teased, the fabric bags she'd brought bulging with stuff.

"Check him out." She showed off the two pictures, one blurry russet blob and the other a distinct muzzle, eyes, and ears.

Poppy enlarged it. "He is big," she muttered. "We should go. It's about to rain."

The first drop hit Meadow on the nose, and she laughed. "Psychic!"

"More like a princess who doesn't like to get wet. Last one to the house is a rotten egg!" Poppy chirped.

They quickly gathered Meadow's things then ran for the house. Meadow lost by quite a bit.

Despite being soaked by the time she reached a dry Poppy under the verandah, she was laughing. "That was refreshing."

"You should get changed. But first, can you send me the pic of that fox? I want to show Darian."

"Sure."

The image went off with a ping, and since Amarok wasn't home, Meadow used his room to change. Dressed only in her bra and panties, she had her arms in the air, shirt half over her face, when the door opened.

"Uh." Was the grunt she heard.

"Sorry. I thought I locked it."

"Doesn't work right." Rok's gruff reply.

She tugged the shirt over her head. It fell to her hips, hiding most of her, and yet his gaze remained smoldering. "I got caught in the rain."

"I see that." He took a step forward, shutting the door behind him.

Her heart raced.

He stopped in front of her, and she had to look up.

"Hi." She could think of nothing else to say.

Apparently, neither could he because his mouth was against hers. He kissed her suddenly. Fiercely. With tongue that curled her toes.

The knock on the door and Poppy's yelled, "Hot cocoa and cookies in the kitchen," froze him.

They stared at each other. Her lips throbbed. Her pussy was wet.

He set Meadow on her feet. "I need to go."

What he needed to do was finish what he started.

He didn't.

Lucky for her, Poppy had chocolate.

THIRTEEN

WHY DID HE KISS HER? ROK WANTED TO BANG his head off a wall. In his defense, he'd been caught off guard. He'd opened the door with a firm twist when it stuck. Seeing her, curvy and delicious, was too tempting to resist.

Had Poppy not knocked, he might not have stopped at just kissing.

He stalked into the kitchen, snagged a cookie. Knowing Poppy, they were hot from the oven.

The gooey goodness didn't disappoint, so he grabbed a second one from the plate and had it halfway to his mouth when Darian entered saying, "Wallace is gone."

Rather than reply, he ate the cookie.

"Did you hear me?"

Rok swallowed and eyed a third. "I heard you

and am wondering why it's a big deal. The man is always going off somewhere. You know he likes the woods."

Wallace, in his sixties, had begun eschewing social company of late. His mate was more than two decades dead now. A hunter got her, and they never had kids. Alone for this long left him untethered. Less in control. He'd been showing feral tendencies of late. Snapping for less and less cause. Looking for an excuse to be in fur not skin. Wallace had even taken to sleeping on a hammock outside most nights, claiming his room was too stifling.

"It's been a week."

"That's long for him."

Usually, the fur excursions were three to five days at a time before Wallace craved some of Poppy's cooking. At the same time, Rok knew one day Wallace wouldn't come back and there'd be a lone wolf running the land, howling at the sky.

What if the old man was in trouble, though? Hurt somewhere?

"Where are his last tracks?" Rok asked, losing the fight with the third cookie.

"A couple yards off the raspberry bush." No need for Darian to elucidate the fact he meant the same bush that was pissed on.

Rok's jaw clenched. "Think he might have seen

who did it?" Given that person wanted to remain anonymous for the moment, did that mean bad things for Wallace?

"Your guess is as good as mine." Darian shrugged just as Poppy joined them, glancing over her shoulder up the hall.

Rok could have told her Meadow had yet to come out of his room. He remained attuned to her in a way that didn't bode well for his single-life prospects.

The very idea she might be the one. The one to soften him. Tame him. Keep him from turning into a bastard like his father.

"Why does your face look like you sucked a lemon? Did I mess up the cookies?" Poppy exclaimed, and he had to quickly cover.

"Delicious. Just worried you'll smack me for eating them all." He grabbed a fourth.

Poppy slapped his hand. "Enough for you. Save some for others."

"What if I don't want to?" Rok teased. Poppy was the little sister he never had, and he'd developed a teasing rapport with her.

Only she wasn't smiling. "There might be a problem. Your girlfriend saw something down by the creek."

"She's not my girlfriend."

"That's the part you're going to focus on?" Darian snorted. "Jeezus do you have it bad."

Had what? She was just a woman he was attracted to. She was leaving in less than a week. And she'd yet to come out of the bedroom. She probably needed time to cool down. They'd both been pretty hot and bothered.

Poppy dumped a cold bucket on that thought. "Yes, he does, and not the point. There was an animal down by the creek. Now mind, I didn't see anything, but Meadow got a picture and showed me. It looked like a cross between a fox and a wolf."

"Impossible. Foxes don't have the right number of chromosomes to mate with a wolf." Rok had learned much about animals and the whole procreation thing when his uncle took him on as heir to his ranch.

"I know that, and you know that, but look." Poppy whipped out her phone. "Tell me what this is then."

The blend of fox and wolf appeared seamless. Fox coloring. Wolf size and eyes. "Are you sure it's authentic?"

"Why would Meadow lie?"

"Could be related to the intruder who's been playing games," Darian opined.

"Now you're stretching. I highly doubt this

image is real. Maybe Meadow is hoping to go viral so she Photoshopped something. It would explain why only she saw it."

"She wouldn't do that." Poppy instantly defended her.

Deep down, he didn't think she would either, and yet the image made no sense. "I'll talk to her." He turned and saw Meadow coming down the hall.

"What about Wallace?" Darian asked in a low tone.

"I doubt he's still on the property given we've seen no traces. He's probably in the park." A massive provincial one practically next door. "Let's see what the forestry folks are chattering about. Has anyone reported a wolf?"

"Might be time to rethink the no electronic monitoring ban," Darian pointed out.

"I am not making anyone wear a tracker," he growled. They'd argued about this before.

"Fine, but you could at least let me put in some cameras. If we had them, we could have known what direction Wallace went."

"The old bastard is tough. I'm sure he's fine." But they wouldn't be if it turned out he was just relaxing and they interrupted him. "Zip it. She's here."

"Which is our cue to leave," Darian declared,

grabbing his sister by the hand. "Come check the goats with me."

"But..." Poppy eyed Rok then Meadow. She smiled.

Fuck.

Poppy pointed. "Her hot cocoa is in the white mug. There's more in the pot for a second since she shouldn't be drinking it alone."

"What are you trying to do?"

"Me? Just helping you out." She winked at Rok.

"I don't need help." Rok glared at Poppy. Her grin widened with mischief, better than trembling like when she first got here, afraid of her own shadow.

"Have fun," she sang as she sailed out the back door.

Meadow arrived with a chirped, "Where did everyone go?"

"Apparently, they had shit to do," he muttered, his hot gaze on Meadow. Mistake. He flashed to her in her bra and panties. The perfect flesh of her inviting. "You look drier."

"I, um, am?" she said in a lilting tone.

"Are you?" he purred, his eyes half shuttering as his gaze dipped to the vee between her legs.

He could smell her arousal.

She wants me.

Fuck, I want her.

"Someone said something about chocolate," she huffed, her cheeks turning pink. Her movements jerky, she slipped to the other side of the island and sipped her hot cocoa.

He wanted to lick the faint froth off her lips.

He had to focus.

"Poppy showed me a picture you took of a fox. Where was it taken?"

"Down by the creek. About a five-minute hike from the dam."

A place he'd recently passed through and not scented anything out of the ordinary. "Don't lie."

"Why would I lie?" Her brow creased.

"Is this about raising the popularity of your blog?" The accusation spilled harshly from his lips.

"The blog is about Weaver. I doubt I'll put up that picture of the fox. They're not that rare you know. We even get them in the city."

"It's not a fox."

"Of course, it is." She rolled her eyes. "I was there. I saw it. Red fur equals fox. See." She held out her phone and enlarged the image.

"That's not a fox."

She squinted. "Guess it could be a dog with unique coloring."

"Or a wolf."

"What makes you say that?"

"The size for one. The eyes. The ears."

"The color is all wrong for a wolf, though."

"Mmm." He hummed. Distracted by the smell of her, he wanted to bury his nose in her hair and nuzzle the fuck out of her.

"It can't be a wolf-fox hybrid. They're impossible. Then again, could be they're like a rare Hinny. You know a stallion and a female donkey mating."

"Not that rare given the number of mules in the world."

"You're thinking of a mare and a jack, a male. It's less common the other way because of a chromosome discrepancy. The one between fox and wolf is more severe. It's why a mixture has never been documented." She was well informed and dug her own grave.

"Making that image a fake!" he accused.

She stared at him. "Do you really think I'd do that?"

"You just admitted a hybrid is impossible.

"It is, which means the picture I took obviously has some kind of trick of the light happening. I would certainly never make something up. What kind of person do you think I am?"

"I don't know other than you showed up here out of the blue and now you're sleeping in my bed." It came out harsh, and she recoiled.

"Excuse me, but I never asked to be given your room. I was perfectly happy sleeping outside."

"Bullshit. No one camps without a tent. You knew I'd invite you inside. You manipulated me." The words left his lips, and he wanted to immediately retract them because they weren't true. That level of subterfuge wasn't Meadow.

Too late, though.

The shock on her expression didn't cover the pain at his accusation. "You know, if you didn't want me here, you could have just said so. You don't need to make baseless accusations. Since my presence is obviously bothersome to you, I'll leave."

"Good." He doubled down because ultimately that was for the best. She would go and he'd be free of the turmoil she caused. The temptation she posed.

Keep her.

He kept his hands behind his back as she headed for his room. Probably to grab her things. He went outside and pretended to do yard cleanup, his senses attuned for the moment the front door opened.

He didn't realize he was hugging the corner of the house until he heard the crunch of gravel, the hydraulic as her trunk opened, the slam as it shut.

The engine started. She didn't come looking for him. Didn't ask him to stay. Obviously wasn't struggling like he was. His fingers dug so hard into the siding it splintered.

Don't leave.

The car's pitch changed as she put it into gear.

As she moved away—*Leaving me!*—he couldn't stop the eruption of a mournful howl.

FOURTEEN

Meadow might be bold and forward in some things, but she wasn't one to beg. While clearly conflicted, Rok made it clear he didn't want her there. One minute hot and eager to pleasure, the next cold and accusing her of faking an image.

As if she'd ever stoop to doing that. She'd not even noticed the fox might be something else until he pointed it out.

It must have been some trick of the light that gave the fox wolfish traits. Or was it a wolf who just appeared too red and narrow nosed? Who cared? She didn't.

Tell that to her white knuckles on the steering wheel.

"Oooh!" she yelled. "That man makes me so mad." Mad. Wet. Intrigued. Sad.

It wasn't just losing her chance with Weaver that bothered her but Rok's rejection. He didn't want her. The passion she'd thought so special between them was obviously one sided.

It made her wonder what traumatized him. Both Poppy and Astra alluded to something in his past. Something horrible enough he would rather be miserable.

Pity, because he had a lot to offer to a woman. And she had a lot to offer to any man who finally looked past her extra pounds and tendency to talk non-stop.

The dating field in her case resembled more a dog park sprinkled with smelly surprises. The guys she dated had no interest in her work at the sanctuary, and the one fellow who did seem keen had a fetish for mating documentaries of animals. They turned him on, and he always had to finish from behind. It was when he slapped her ass and told her to giddy up that she ended things.

Rok had an interest in nature that so far stayed away from creepy. He also showed a protective instinct she found crazy sexy. But he was also insanely moody.

A broken man. She kept reminding herself she wasn't the glue to fix him, but as she drove away, she wished she could be. She'd seen how he could be with his friends. Caring, funny, sweet. He'd make some woman very lucky.

A woman not named Meadow.

Sigh.

The wipers on her car went double time. The rain still came down steadily, the day gray and dreary. Everything was sopping wet. She took it easy with the speed knowing how slick the pavement could get. She'd also read more than a few articles about the dangers of wildlife and traffic. With her small car, even a raccoon in her path would be fatal.

Lights flashed in her rearview mirror. A glance showed a vehicle riding up her tail.

The road ended at the ranch. Someone had come after her.

Rok?

Curse her heart for beating faster. As if she cared. She did. She totally did, which was why she began to slow down, her gaze flicking to the rearview mirror, not paying attention in front. It was only by chance she realized something suddenly crossed in front of her.

A man bolted across the road, naked, with his gray hair streaming. She slammed on the brakes. The car skidded on the wet pavement and then spun, whipping her side to side before it flung itself off the road and into a tree.

FIFTEEN

Meadow's brake lights suddenly came on. She'd seen him and was slowing—

"Fuck!"

Her car suddenly spun out of control. Nothing to be done but watch as that ridiculous toy of hers slammed into a tree. And the winner of that encounter?

Not the driver.

Meadow!

The seconds separating them took forever. The moment he slammed the truck into park, he was piling out the door and scrabbling to her car. The air bag filled the front, but her head lay against the glass window of the driver's side door. Blood streaked down from her temple.

Fuck. Fuck. Fuck.

This was his fault. Making baseless accusations because this woman scared him. The moment she'd left he'd berated himself. Howled at his cowardice before finally moving his ass to go after her. With that tiny car of hers, she wouldn't have gotten far. Just far enough to get in trouble apparently.

He yanked open the door and grabbed her so she wouldn't fall. She moaned, and he growled as he cradled her.

Her lashes fluttered. "Rok." Not a question, more of a sighing relief.

"I'm here, Doe." He shortened her name as he stroked the hair from her face, noticing the blood came from a shallow cut an inch below her hairline. He checked her for more damage as he murmured some more to keep her focused on him. "I didn't know you were into stunt driving."

"There was a man," she muttered. "A naked man. Ran in front of my car."

The assertion startled. He'd not seen anything, but then again, she'd been far ahead still, the misty air making only the bright red of her taillights clear. And to be honest, he wasn't looking at anything else.

"I didn't see anyone."

"Not lying," she insisted. "Saw him."

It hurt that she thought he accused her again. "I believe you."

"Find him. Needs help."

"I'll bet he does," was his grumble. But it wouldn't be from Rok. He wasn't about to leave an injured Meadow to go looking, not when he had a good idea who she'd seen.

"What are you doing?" she asked as he scooped her into his arms.

"Taking you somewhere warm and more spacious."

"Your truck is an enemy of the environment."

"Tell that to your ready-for-the-scrap-heap car. How much do you think that will cost the earth?" Arguing with a woman with a head injury. What was wrong with him?

She uttered a small chuckle. "Guess I won't win this one."

"If it makes you feel better, we're a zero-waste ranch. We try to use everything."

"Wish I could have stuck around long enough to learn about it," she mumbled, her head lolling against his chest.

"No sleeping, Doe." Or should he let her slumber? He couldn't remember the latest advice on head injuries. It had changed a few times. He placed her in the front seat of his truck and reclined it as far back as he could before strapping her in.

Her lashes fluttered. "It is warm. Smells like you."

He froze.

"Not a bad thing. I swear." She uttered an embarrassed laugh.

He'd never thought it was. "Let's get you back to the ranch."

"Before we go, can you grab the bag on the front seat? I might need a pair of pants. Pretty sure I peed myself a bit."

She had. Hell, he'd peed himself a bit when he saw her hit that tree.

While he wanted to race back to the ranch to get her patched up, he couldn't deny her request. The problem being there were a lot of bags in her car, so he grabbed as many as would fit in his back seat, which wasn't quite everything. The woman had epically packed that thing.

As he slammed the doors shut on the car that would never drive again, given its twisted frame, he caught a flash of russet. A quick turn of his head and he captured the bushy red and white of a tail.

Fox colors, if too large, reminding him of the picture she'd taken. Could it actually be real?

He got in the truck, and she managed a wan, "Sorry about denting your tree."

"Tree's fine. Your car, though... I'll have it towed to the house."

"It might be a little bit broken."

"A little?" He snorted. "Speaking of broken, you appear cohcrent, which is good. How's the head?"

"Ouchy. I ricocheted off the side glass."

"You've got a cut, but you won't need stitches. We've got the tape and glue to shut it for you."

"Guess living out here, you'd need to know some first aid."

"Hospital is kind of far. How's the rest of you feel?"

"Okay for now. I imagine the whiplash will hit later." She grimaced. "At least I didn't hit him."

A reminder of what she'd claimed earlier. "You saw a man. Would you say older? Long gray hair?"

She didn't reply. He glanced over to see her eyes shut. Fuck. "Wake up." Not a twitch.

Pedal to the floor, Rok drove quickly back to the ranch, juggling driving while texting ahead to Bellamy to be ready. As their resident vet, he was the one in charge of patching them up when injured—which was often—and handling the livestock ailments.

He left her shit in the back to carry her into the house yelling, "Bellamy."

"Kitchen," was the answering holler.

Injuries with blood were taken care of in the one room that could be sprayed and wiped down without permanent staining.

This was his fault. He'd sent Doe away. She got hurt because of him.

"Your mother died because of you." His father's oft-stated claim echoed.

"What happened?" Astra asked as he entered the kitchen and laid Meadow on the counter. Her eyes were still closed.

"Road's slick on account of the rain. She had to brake abruptly because an old naked guy ran across in front of her."

"Wallace," Astra surmised.

Had to be. Who else would be running around in his birthday suit in the woods?

"He finally went over the edge," Rok agreed. Meaning they'd have to hunt Wallace down and secure him. It would be one thing for him to be feral in wolf form. So long as he didn't hurt people, he could live a life in the wild. However, a feral naked human running around would draw the wrong kind of attention.

"How long has she been unconscious?" Bellamy asked, palpating Meadow's ribs and abdomen while Astra cleaned and glued the cut on her forehead shut.

"Only a few minutes. She started out talking to me and then nothing."

"Meadow, can you open your eyes for me?" Bellamy talked softly and held open her eyelids to shine a light.

She grumbled. "Too bright."

"How do you feel?" Bellamy asked.

"Like I hit a tree."

Astra chuckled. "And lost by the sounds of it."

Meadow groaned. "My poor Ladybug."

"Got squashed. You'll need to call your insurance." Rok didn't mean to sound so gruff.

"Ugh. Not yet." She turned to eye him. "Someone needs to find the man."

"Already on it, Doe." His voice softened. "You rest. I'll handle everything."

"Hard to rest with the throb in my head. I don't suppose I can have some Tylenol?"

"Bellamy?" Rok eyed his friend.

"One to take off the edge. You might have a concussion, meaning if you feel nauseous, or worse, you need to tell someone right away."

"I didn't whack my head that hard."

"You passed out," Rok reminded.

"Because I'm a wimp about pain. I'll probably pass out again if I don't get something for the throbbing."

Rok held her up as Astra gave her a pill and water to wash it down. As he swung her into his arms, Bellamy had more instructions.

"While I didn't feel anything internally, let me know if you get any twinges."

"I will," Meadow promised.

"Nothing strenuous for at least the next twenty-four hours. And someone needs to wake her every two hours."

"I'll handle it," Rok volunteered.

"You don't have to," was her soft murmur. "I can put a timer on my phone."

His reply? A growl and a firm stalk from the kitchen for his room.

"I'm not sleeping in your bed." She went from scaring him to pissing him off.

"You are."

"No, I'm not. Give me the couch. We both know I fit better on it than you."

"You're sleeping in my bed, and that's final."

"I won't have you accuse me of manipulating my way into it again."

Shame hit him. Meaning he owed her an apology. "I shouldn't have said that."

"But you did."

"And now I'm sorry. So zip it."

"You can't tell me to shut up just because you apologized."

Why not? It would make things easier. Then again, did he deserve easier? "Can't you forget I was an asshole and go back to happy Meadow?"

"Why?"

"Don't you want to be happy?"

"No, I mean, why were you an asshole?"

Awkward question. He placed her on his bed while he thought of an answer.

Okay he was trying to think of a plausible lie, only to realize lying was why she was injured in his bed. "I was a dick because I like you." Understatement but the only thing he could put clearly into words.

"You like me, so you're mean to me," she repeated slowly.

He winced. "I know it sounds backwards." Like a boy who yanked on braids in school.

A smile spread across her face. "Actually, it makes perfect sense, Rocky. You feel something for me, and it frightens, so you lash out rather than deal with it."

His lips twisted. "I'm a coward."

"You're human."

On that account she was wrong. She'd yet to ask why they'd never offered to take her to a hospital.

Not that it was an option. First, it was more than forty minutes away. And second, the ranch kept off the radar. Bringing in an injured woman wouldn't go unnoticed. Especially if she woke up talking of streaking men in the woods. Their secret must be kept at all costs. A harsh reality that had him pressing his lips tight and hoping she would be fine.

She had to be. It couldn't happen again.

You killed your mother.

The echo of the past wouldn't stop its taunting. Especially since it was his fault Meadow almost died, too.

Perhaps he was cursed to be alone.

SIXTEEN

ROK DIDN'T LEAVE HER ALONE FOR A MINUTE, and Meadow couldn't get enough of his presence.

Despite the throb in her head, she was in great spirits, and that was due to Rok's efforts. Since Bellamy suggested no television or reading, and lights made her headache worse, Rok kept her company, reading aloud to her from a book he'd chosen at random. A murder mystery that put her to sleep, leaning against him.

When she woke before the first two-hour mark, it was to find him sitting with his eyes closed in a chair placed alongside the bed.

"Why do you look sad?" she mused aloud, only to realize he wasn't asleep.

He eyed her, a slight frown on his brow. "Not sad. It's nothing."

"Is it?" She forged ahead. "Your friends seem to think you're grumpy because of your past."

"My friends should keep their mouths shut."

"They did," she hastened to say. "They only alluded to it so I wouldn't be tempted to club you over the head for being stubborn and grouchy all the time."

"You wouldn't hurt a fly."

"True." Her lips twisted ruefully. "Not going to deny the stubborn and grouchy part?"

His shoulders rolled. "Not much point since it's true."

"Why?"

For a second, she thought he wouldn't reply. When he did, it emerged so softly she almost missed it. "I didn't have a good childhood."

"What happened?"

Sorrow tugged at his features, and she wanted to reach out and stroke it away.

"I don't talk about my past."

"Oh, Rocky. Ever think it might help if you did?"

"Not really. Only person who kind of knew what happened to me was my uncle. And he used to say best to forget it and move on."

"How's that working for you?"

His lips twisted into a wry smile. "You saying my uncle's advice was wrong?"

"Have you forgotten and moved on?"

"If I say yes, you'll call me a liar. If I say no, then you'll bug me about it."

"Bug?" she riposted. "It's called sharing. Being honest with each other."

"What if I'm not ready?"

"Then don't." She thought that would be the end of it, but he fidgeted.

"If I tell you, it will sound like I'm whining."

"Given where you are now in life, it will be more like a story of your victory over adversity."

He froze. "What do you mean?"

"You had a bad childhood but look at you now. A successful rancher with all kinds of friends supporting you while living in paradise."

His lips quirked. "When you put it like that... Guess I did all right."

"Better than all right."

"Only because of my uncle. He took me in when I had nowhere to go."

"Did your parents die?" That would have been traumatic.

"My mom did, and my dad blamed me for it."

Her heart ached for him because he tried to sound blasé—and failed. "I'm sorry to hear that. What happened?"

"She gave birth to me." A bitter laugh emerged. "I killed her. Not even a minute old and a murderer."

It took a second for her to blurt out, "Sounds as if she died of a medical emergency, and that's not your fault."

"According to my dad it was. After my birth, he wouldn't have anything to do with me. He shunted me to my aunts until the age of three. That was when I accidentally came to his notice. Earned my first beating and since my aunts were obviously not teaching me discipline, he took me back so he could have a firm hand in my upbringing." No need to elucidate.

"Oh no." She breathed the two syllables with a breaking heart. It horrified her to know people that evil existed in the world.

"At sixteen I'd had enough. He told me to get out, so I left and never looked back."

"I can see why you have issues with trust and intimacy." He was broken.

He grimaced. "I trust just fine."

"You accused me of faking a pic for social media attention and maneuvering you into being a free hotel."

The flinch went well with his wince. "I fucked up."

"You did. So now you fix it."

"How?"

"Don't do it again."

"And?"

"And I'd say that's the best start."

"No, because that's not punishment. I need to atone." He bristled and jumped up to pace, his body a live wire of tension.

"Calm down. I don't want anything from you."

For some reason that had him freezing. "I need to go out."

Nothing more. He just left. Good because she was feeling tired again. Her head throbbed too much to deal with Rok right now.

She must have dozed off because, next thing she knew, he nudged her awake. "Open your eyes, Doe. Let's hear you talk." He tapped her lightly on the cheek.

She grimaced and squinted. "Princes usually kiss instead of slap."

"Hardly a prince," he said on a low chuckle.

"Yet you saved me again." She turned her head and saw the blanket kicked to the side by the chair. "You better not be sleeping in that chair."

"It's fine."

"It is not fine. Get in this bed, right now, Rocky."

"You need to rest."

"I can rest just fine sharing your bed. Or would you prefer I go sleep on the couch?"

"You're not sleeping on the couch."

"I will if you don't get in bed with me," she obstinately insisted.

"Why must you argue?"

She grinned. "Because it's the only way to get you to stop being stubborn. Now stop stalling. Bed." She lifted the cover and scooched to give him room.

His expression turned wary. "Why are you so nice to me? We both know I've been a dick."

"More like socially awkward."

"I am not awkward." He couldn't hide his offense.

"Aren't you? Let's see, how many times have you kissed me and run?"

He scowled. "It's complicated."

She couldn't help bubbly laughter. "All relationships are."

"We don't have a relationship."

"Then why did you come after me?" She leaned toward him. "Before I crashed, I saw you in the rearview mirror."

"Coincidence."

"So it wasn't me you were racing to find?"

He said nothing.

She stared.

He shifted uncomfortably. "Okay, I was going after you because turns out maybe I didn't actually want you to go."

Her lips curved. "Would it help if I said I didn't want to leave either?" There was something about him she couldn't seem to resist.

"I'm sorry."

"You said that." And she believed him. "Come to bed."

He peeled off his sweater and said, "I really didn't mean what I said."

"Which part? Because I thought you said something about liking me."

"That part's true." He sat on the edge of the bed. The mattress must be of excellent quality because she didn't move. "But I don't want you to feel obliged to like me back."

"I don't feel obliged to do anything." His sense of honor ran a little too deep. She patted the spot next to her. "But I would like to snuggle."

"How can you want to be near me when it's my fault you had an accident?"

He genuinely blamed himself. Felt as if he needed punishment. "You want someone to blame, then blame the naked man running across the road. Did anyone ever find him?"

He shrugged. "Hard to find anything in the rainy dark."

"Well, I hope you try in the morning because it was super creepy. Are pervs in the woods why Poppy's so nervous all the time?"

"Wallace would never hurt Poppy."

"Wait, you know the naked guy?"

"Pretty sure it's Wallace. He went missing a few days ago. He's usually harmless. Guess that's changed. We'll find him." He sounded so grim.

Probably thought he was to blame for this Wallace person going crazy. He needed to relax. She sat up and put her hands on his shoulders.

He stiffened. "What are you doing?"

"Trying to knead your stiff muscles." It was like massaging a rock.

He dragged her onto his lap. "There's only one stiff thing that needs your attention." And it pressed against her bottom.

Her breath caught. "Oh. That is hard." Horrible innuendo talk, and yet her heart fluttered.

His fingers dug into her ass as he shifted her, applying pressure well enough she caught her bottom lip.

His eyes shimmered for a moment in the murky room.

She leaned forward and kissed him. He trembled

as her mouth slid over his with a sensuality that sped up her pulse. When her tongue tickled the seam of his lips, he groaned.

"I need to go."

"Right away?" She clutched his shoulders and rocked in his lap.

He sucked in a breath. "Doe, you're still recovering. We need to stop. I should have never started."

"I started," she chuckled, leaning in to nip his chin. "I think I know what I'm capable of." Her head barely ached, but other parts of her...

"You make it hard to do the right thing."

"Are you going to tell me the right thing is you leaving instead of having sex?"

"You're injured."

"Sexual endorphins are excellent pain blockers." She brushed her mouth against his.

"Fuck." A gruff word.

"I'd like to."

SEVENTEEN

Meadow drove him wild. Her every word was innuendo laced. Her actions pure seduction. She rocked lightly, applying pressure on them both. The good kind. She ignored his lips to bite his ear lobe, tugging it and blowing hotly until he hissed, his fingers digging into her hips.

"Do you like that?" She smiled at him, teasing.

Did she grasp the effect she had on him? She weakened his resolve. His knees. His arguments.

He wanted her like nothing he'd wanted before. And in a miracle, she wanted him, too.

Her lips hovered in front of his. "Maybe a proper kiss would fix me."

Only forever might fix him.

He dragged her close and pressed his mouth to hers. Embraced her hard. Deep. Kept his hands on her hips and ground her against him as their mouths melded in the hottest of embraces.

For a second, he forgot she was injured. Forgot Wallace still ran around in the woods. It was all about Meadow. The taste of her. The feel. The scent. The need...

He had to be responsible, even if it killed him. He reluctantly pulled free. "We can't do this right now. You heard Bellamy. Twenty-four hours of nothing strenuous."

She rubbed her nose against his as she purred, "I'm okay with you doing all the work."

He just about fucking fell off the bed. He was tempted. So very tempted. "What if I read to you instead?"

"That involves light," she grumbled. "I'd rather just hear you talk."

"About what?"

"Tell me about the alpacas."

"Seriously?"

"Yup. Tell me about those cuties." She snuggled into him.

Rather than pace and wait for news of those searching for Wallace, he held Doe in his lap and talked.

And it wasn't one sided. He started by stiltedly telling her about the first time he met an alpaca and how it spit on him. She laughed too hard. He tried a more serious story next. She still snickered and regaled him with her own tales of woe, which had him chuckling.

He found out Meadow had never been to an actual tropical beach, just the one off the British Columbia coast. She could swim but didn't like opening her eyes under water. She also hated the feel of moss.

She talked a mile a minute, and he absorbed it all with grunts in the right spots and a few anecdotes of his own. When she finally stopped to take a breath and exclaim, "I'm boring you, aren't I?" he quite honestly said, "You could never bore me."

The truth and not one he meant to admit. Her eyes widened, and her fingers skimmed over his cheek. "You're pretty interesting yourself."

"There's things about me you don't understand."

"Because you're complicated. I am starting to get that. But if it helps, I'm a good listener."

"Give me time," was all he could say. Time to figure out what he felt and what to do about it. Because Meadow was human. One hundred percent. Which meant uncertainty when it came to how she'd deal with his secret. If they mated, it would only be a matter of time before she found out. Before that happened, she'd have to be Oath Bound.

Something that required an Alpha to preside over. But who to ask?

Amarok belonged nowhere and had no ties to any pack. Any request to bind a human would draw attention to not just him but the ranch and the Weres who depended on him. Trusted him to keep them safe. Having Meadow here could jeopardize everything, but at the same time, he couldn't let her go.

She fell asleep in his lap, and he stayed with her, waking her every few hours as he was supposed to despite her grumbled complaints.

In the morning, she woke and squirmed against him. At first innocently, then with erotic intention.

He sucked in a breath. "Morning."

"Mmm." Her husky greeting as she shifted again and nuzzled him.

"How are you feeling?" he asked.

"Horny." Said with a naughty chuckle.

"We should probably wait. Make sure your concussion is better."

"I don't even have headache." She kissed her way up his neck.

He closed his eyes and clenched his fists. "I don't think I'll be able to stop."

"Good." She nipped the lobe of his ear, and he

groaned. "I'm feeling like celebrating the fact I'm alive."

"We really should have you checked over first."

"Later. I want you inside me," she whispered.

He groaned. He found her mouth with his for a kiss that had them both panting and aching.

He lay her on his bed, half covering her, his hands moving to remove her clothes when someone knocked at the door.

"Go away."

Lochlan's reply had him rolling out of bed. "We found Wallace."

EIGHTEEN

Forget sexy times. Meadow didn't say a word as Rok left the bedroom. What could she say to ease his grim expression? He looked as if someone had died.

Wait, had Wallace died? She didn't have a chance to ask; he departed too quickly.

She showered and dressed, feeling fine if she ignored the cut and bruise on the side of her head. Her body felt good, and while a little sore, her neck didn't have the feared whiplash.

Pulling the curtains open, she could see the day remained dreary, the rain coming down heavy. That didn't stop Rok from standing outside in it. She could see him by the edge of the woods, waiting. A sentinel with hunched shoulders.

She headed to the kitchen with its smell of hot

coffee and baking. Poppy stood behind the counter, whisking and pouring and flipping. Making mounds of food to handle her anxiety.

"Morning." Meadow didn't say good because it so obviously wasn't.

"There's fresh coffee in the pot, and I've got a batch of cinnamon rolls I'm about to ice. Unless you'd prefer something else? I can do eggs and bacon."

"The rolls sound delish." Meadow poured a coffee and seated herself, the first pungent sip pure delight. None of that capsule stuff here. Only freshly ground beans that enticed the senses.

Poppy slid a plate with a hot bun slathered in icing in front of her. "Breakfast of champions."

"Good god that's delicious." Meadow couldn't help but moan.

"I thought everyone could use something decadent. It's going to be a long day."

"I take it Wallace isn't okay?"

Poppy shook her head. Her lips turned down. "He's dead."

"I'm sorry. Were you close?"

"No, but then again, no one really was. He's been at the ranch since before any of us. Got here about a decade after his wife died. Kept a lot to himself. Especially recently."

"Sounds like he was depressed." It explained why he jumped in front of her car. She'd avoided his suicide attempt, but apparently he still found a way.

"You could say. I know he missed his mate. Wife," Poppy quickly corrected. "Without her, it just became harder and harder for him to connect with people. He had no interest."

"Sounds like he loved her very much."

"He did."

They were both quiet for a moment as the roar of the side-by-side filled the air. It rolled into the yard with a large canvas bundle tied to the back and slowed as it came abreast of Rok.

Meadow frowned. "It looks like they brought back the body."

"They couldn't exactly leave it in the woods."

"Don't the cops want you to leave it at the scene so they can be sure it wasn't foul play?"

Poppy shook her head. "We don't bother the police for natural causes. We call it in and then bury them."

"What about his family?"

"We are his family."

Poppy turned somber as they watched Rok escort the trundling ATV toward the massive garage where Nova waited by the open bay door. Beyond it was the flash of red. Her car. It had been towed to the ranch and stored until the insurance was dealt with it. As the door closed, it hit her hard. Had her reflexes been slower, she would have been the one to kill him.

She swallowed hard. "I need some air."

"It's raining," Poppy reminded.

But she needed outside. "Just for a few minutes. I won't go far." She headed for the front door and stuck her head out, breathing deep. In. Out.

It wasn't enough. She felt dizzy. The shock finally hit her.

I almost died.

Heck, for all she knew, she *had* killed Wallace. What if their close encounter led to him having a heart attack? Or in his panic, he ran off a cliff or—

She hyperventilated. Panic filled her, as she couldn't help but wonder, was she at fault?

Desperate for fresh air, she dressed in her slicker and boots left by the entrance. Someone must have found them when they emptied her car. A car that was now scrap metal. It was a wonder she'd walked away.

She headed outside, protected somewhat by the porch's overhang. Moist air kissed her skin. She closed her eyes as she inhaled deep, centering herself. Calming her anxiety with the soothing pitter-patter of rain. It poured steadily, long enough that runnels of water snaked through the front yard and across the driveway. Too much for the ground to absorb.

How fared Weaver in this weather? Rok had warned of the creek before this dumping of moisture. Had the dam survived?

She had to know. The exercise would be good for her. She headed for the creek, using the muddy trail. The woods didn't offer much protection. The leaves only served to pool the rain until they tilted and poured in thick, wet runs. The one that managed to find its way down her neck especially chilled. She almost turned back, but then again, getting wet for a few more minutes wouldn't make a difference. She was almost there.

The roar of rushing water hit her ears before the sight of it. She gaped to see the creek had swelled well past its banks, the current strong enough to hurtle large branches. Muddy grass swirled past.

The violent strength didn't bode well. She paralleled the creek though the woods rather than risk getting close to the flowing edge. It wouldn't take much to get sucked in. She'd not survived one death to fall victim to another. She'd seen *Final Destination* and knew better than to tempt the Reaper.

The spattering rain lessened as the clouds overhead offered a reprieve. She picked her way to the spot where Weaver had been building. His home with its many branches and a few slim trunks held steady to the edge of a widening lake. His dam appeared to be causing a backlog of water.

Keeping an eye on the ground with it treacherous slick spots, she got closer, hoping to get a peek of Weaver. Was he snug in his home? Safe?

The reprieve from the storm ended. The rain chose to come down harder, a reminder to get her ass back inside. Meadow had not told anyone she was coming down here. She'd hate for anyone to get worried. Rok especially. He was already dealing with enough.

Meadow whirled to head back, only to gasp as she discovered a man standing mere feet from her. Dressed in loose pants—wet and stained, same as his shirt—and barefoot, his feet caked in mud. His features were old, his hair a dripping gray mess that hung down his back.

The man she almost killed on the road bared yellowed teeth and said, "Where do you think you're going?"

NINETEEN

THE SIDE-BY-SIDE DRIPPED ON THE CONCRETE.
Rok and the others stood around it, silent.

Hammer spoke first. "He was an ornery old
bastard, but a hard worker."

At that they all nodded.

"That man always came home with at least one
grouse." Usually a few good-sized ones.

"Remember how he called Asher the man
whore."

Said man whore uttered a noise. "Treated me
like a son, he did."

All of their heads drooped, paying their respects
to one who'd passed on.

Now, time to figure out what killed him. Darian
hadn't said shit when he called. Just the basics.
Found Wallace. Bringing him home.

Which meant he thought there was something fishy.

Everyone was in the garage with the exception of Poppy, Astra, and Meadow. Nova undid the knots while Darian paced. Reece and Gary stood side by side and silent. Bellamy readied his tools to examine the body.

With the bindings undone, Rok and Hammer carried Wallace into the workshop area of the garage. The man felt lighter than he should.

"Is it me, or has he lost weight?" The Wallace he knew carried a few extra pounds.

"Animals got to him." Hammer replied.

Rok wasn't alone in wincing. Hopefully the chewing happened well after Wallace died. "You think there's something hinky about his death."

"I know there is," Darian confirmed. "But rather than give you some half-baked shit, I want to see what Bellamy says."

Bellamy took a breath before peeling back the tarp wrapping the body. Nova acted as his assistant as Bellamy studied the corpse. Too small. Too dead.

Fuck.

Rok shoved away from the vehicle and headed for the propane fridge with the beers inside. It was noon somewhere in the world. He handed one to Darian and another to Hammer. Reece shook his head and ran from the garage, Gary following. The man didn't do well with death.

Asher also declined. "I'm going to check on the girls in the house."

Rok almost said no. He didn't want pretty boy near Meadow, but if Wallace had been killed... Better the women have protection until they had a handle on the situation. "Stay with them."

"I'll go, too. I don't need to see this twice." Hammer left with Asher.

Rok turned to Darian. "Tell me everything,"

Clearly shaken, Darren spread his hands. "We found him by accident. Just beyond the border, crammed inside a rock cairn. Might not have found him at all if not for the mudslide. It sheared some of the stone, exposing him."

"Wait, he was buried?"

"Seems like. Those stones were stacked to block the crevice they stuffed him in. We dug Wallace out and brought him home."

"You should have called me sooner," he growled.

"To do what? Besides, you were busy."

He had been. He rubbed the spot between his brows. "You're sure the body you brought back was Wallace?" Because he'd looked at what remained and had a hard time seeing it.

Darian nodded. "Face is mangled, but you can

still see the tattoo on his arm. And he was wearing the shirt Poppy fixed for him."

"Someone buried the body to hide it. Did they kill him?"

"Not sure how he died."

Rok rubbed his bristled chin. "If he was covered in stone, how did he get partially eaten?"

"That's the part I wanted a second opinion on." Darian's expression turned bleak.

Before he could reply, Bellamy muttered, "Fuck me, he was killed."

"What do you mean, killed?" Rok strode over to the workbench draped in a tarp, the body lying atop. Wallace was laid out, the remains in rough condition. His body torn. Chunks missing. The smell of it ripe. As in a few days old.

"This didn't happen recently." He frowned.

"Four or five days at least," Bellamy agreed. "Seems like an animal attack. Wolf by the bite. A big one."

His blood ran cold. "Is it Were?"

"I don't know. Whoever bit him is missing an eye tooth, though."

"Top left?" Rok asked even as he feared the answer.

"Yeah. You know who did this?" Bellamy asked.

Rok's vision turned dark. His lip curled back on a snarl. "My father's here. We need to find him."

"Thought he was an Alpha down in the States somewhere?" Darian queried.

"He is. Meaning if he's here, then he's up to no good."

They all silently glanced at Wallace.

Asher slammed into the garage, wild eyed. "Rok, we might have a problem. Meadow is missing. Poppy thinks she might have gone down to the creek."

Fuck!

TWENTY

THE APPEARANCE OF THE OLD MAN STARTLED
Meadow. She clutched her chest. "Goodness, you
scared me."

"Of course, you're scared. You're human." He
sneered, as if it were an insult.

"Better than being a worm." She smiled, trying to
make it sound amusing.

He didn't seem amused. "You don't belong here."
His craggy features wrinkled in disapproval.

"I'm actually a guest at the ranch. White Wolf
Ranch," she specified. "Did I accidentally wander off
their property?" She'd have sworn this entire area
belonged to them.

"White Wolf Ranch." He spat on the ground.
"You know Amarok?"

"I do. Such a nice man."

More spit hit the ground. "He's a fucking disappointment. Takes after his mother."

"Oh, you knew his parents?"

His lip lifted. "I *am* his parent. To my fucking shame."

"You're Rok's dad?" She didn't see much resemblance. Nor did she like his attitude.

"I doubt that shit's spoken of me. It's been a while since we've seen each other."

"What a shame. My parents live on the coast these days because mom hates those Chinook winds that slide down from the Rockies. Gives her headaches. We try and visit about four five times a year at least. But I understand how circumstance and time can get away from you." She babbled, her go-to when she got nervous.

"I was glad to see him gone. Fuckup needed to toughen up. Why do you think I kicked him out?"

There were so many things a person could reply to such a cold and cruel statement. She arched a brow. "Are you here to ask his forgiveness?"

The man's raucous laughter grated. "More like make him beg for mine."

She recalled what Rok told her about his dad. "He owes you no apology, but from the sounds of it, you do. You were abusive and cruel. An unfit parent."

"You know nothing," he spat.

"You blamed a baby for his mom passing."

"Because he killed her. The doctor told her early on she should abort because she didn't have the right constitution to carry my child. But she wouldn't. He murdered her."

"Wow, do you need help." Muttered aloud before it finally occurred to her she was alone with a very deranged person.

In her defense, this type of crazy shit didn't happen in her world, or in her family. Her dad wasn't a wild-eyed psycho, unless you touched his barbecue. And Mom's idea of violence was whipping cream for dessert.

She angled to the side. The old man continued to watch her, his gaze sharp and menacing.

"I'm surprised the bastard lets a soft skin wander this place. These woods are dangerous." It sounded more threat than warning.

"It was lovely meeting you, sir. I should get back before anyone worries."

"Does anyone even know you're here? Does anyone care? Because I watched them all go into the garage with the dead one. And then you left the house all by your lonesome."

She shivered. "You've been spying on us?"

"Reconnoitering. Learning my enemy."

"He's your son."

"And what is he to you?"

"I'm simply his guest. Perhaps we should go back to the ranch and find him." She wanted the security of Rok's presence. This man screamed danger.

"What are you to my son?" he repeated.

"Nothing. No one."

"Liar. I saw you whoring yourself with him."

Her cheeks pinked. "That must have been uncomfortable for you."

"More like maddening because you'd think he'd have learned his lesson with his mother. She, too, was weak. I knew better than to choose her. And look what happened. She died and left me with a worthless heir."

She couldn't help but defend him. "By the looks of it, he's done quite well without you. He's a successful rancher."

"Is he? Is that why you're sniffing around him? Spreading your legs?"

That went beyond crude. "This is making me uncomfortable. I'm leaving."

He blocked her. "I wonder how upset he'd be if you were to die."

This couldn't be happening. "This isn't funny. Please let me pass."

"Do I look amused?" He had the darkest expression. "I take my killing seriously."

"You're not a killer." Because stating it would make it true.

The old man laughed. "And that's where you're wrong."

He lunged, and she screamed. A shift of her weight and her foot slipped in the slick mud. The clumsiness saved her. He missed, giving her a chance to bolt. The problem being she didn't have many options to flee.

The muddy shore hemmed her in, and when she veered, it cut off the distance between them. The old man slammed into her and grabbed hold of her slicker. She let him keep it and scrabbled away, or at least tried to. The mud of the softened shore gave no traction. She slipped, and he landed atop her, heavy and grunting, fetid and hot despite the cold, clean rain. She struggled, squirming and shifting, only vaguely noticing an approaching roar.

At the last second, he let go of her and sprang off. Meadow choked, gasped for air, and managed to roll on her side before she saw the wall of water rushing down.

The dam must have finally broken.

The water hit like a bomb, sucking the breath from her along with her whole body. The current swept her away from her attacker, not deep but violent enough she couldn't stand up. It was all she could do to get a deep breath during the tumbling and not drown. Forget yelling for help.

She rode the water slide, thankful for one thing. The creek didn't have any big rocks to slam her. When the current eventually ebbed, it spilled her into a forming lake where she managed to grab hold of a tree.

For a second, she breathed. She'd not drowned. Her throat hurt, but she lived.

Which was when she saw the red fur. A flash of it too fast to get any real sense of size or shape.

But the true chill hit at the howl that split the air.

TWENTY-ONE

Rok burst from the garage and howled, a big, broken sound. The moment he heard Meadow was missing he knew.

She's in trouble.

If Samuel truly skulked and had found Meadow, he'd kill her, especially if he'd been watching the house. Even his asshole of a father would recognize Meadow was special to him.

Fuck, how it burned he'd never noticed his father lurking. Samuel was a master of stealth. He'd served in the military for a while. Some kind of special forces. Got kicked out for mental issues. Imagine that. And then was given a pack of his own to abuse because in the Were world might ruled. Alphas, even the ones with violent tendencies, gave the orders.

Darian, the calm and rational one, tried to keep Rok focused. "Let's fan out and head for the creek."

There was nothing calm or fucking rational about this!

Rok tore his shirt even as he ran, consumed by a wild rage. He ignored his friends yelling at him to slow down.

Never.

Only one reason his father would come here.

The time of the final reckoning. A day Rok always knew would come since that first time he stood up to his dad not long after he turned sixteen.

His dad came home drunk. As usual. Rare was the night he didn't have a few. What differed was the level of intoxication. The slam of the door indicated this wasn't the mellow beer kind of drunk.

Bang. Bang. Shoes flew. Shit got slammed around. The worse kind of drunk that came from the golden stuff. Whiskey always turned Samuel mean.

Amarok knew to stay out of his way. Not being noticed kept the beatings at bay.

But his dad was raring for a fight.

Wham. Rok's door slammed open and hit the wall. Samuel stormed into his bedroom, ignoring the fact Rok was abed.

Samuel began ranting. "You lazy fucker. I work

all fucking day and I come home to your lazy entitled ass doing nothing."

Nothing? Amarok's schedule included full-time school plus thirty hours a week split between two jobs, laundry, and any other household chore his father designated while Samuel worked forty at the factory and spent forty more being pissed.

Samuel tore the blanket away, and Amarok rolled to his back annoyed because he had a test in the morning. Math wasn't one of his stronger subjects, and he'd drop it if he could, but the key to getting out of this life was school.

"Go to bed," he muttered to his dad, tired of it already.

"What did you say to me?" His dad fisted his T-shirt and hauled him off the bed.

It had happened for as long as he could remember. They said in school to report bullies. He did at the age of seven. The social workers came and talked to his dad, who lamented about how hard it was to raise a kid on his own, especially one as willful as Amarok. Called him a liar.

When they left, Amarok's father had turned on him. It was so ugly the school thought he almost died of the flu because he stayed home sick for so long waiting for the bruises to fade.

Look away. Don't engage. The rules of survival

beat in his chest, but that day, with his father heaving over him, wild eyed and stinking, Amarok was done with it.

So he shoved. Shoved his father right off him and onto the floor.

Sitting on his ass, Samuel gaped in shock. Amarok's jaw dropped, too.

His father rose with a snarl. "You dare disrespect me?" He puffed his chest to intimidate.

"Leave me alone." Amarok stood from his bed and stretched his lanky frame. When had he gotten taller than his dad?

"Sassing me, fucker?" His dad threatened with two clenched fists.

Rok held his ground. Not just taller, stronger, too. His jobs in the warehouses were building muscle. He crossed those bulky arms and growled. "No more hitting. Don't you ever touch me."

It felt good to say it.

"Disrespectful bastard." His father swung a fist.

He caught it. "I said no hit—"

Oof.

As if Samuel would be so easily cowed. He gut-punched, but Amarok blocked the follow up. Then he began landing a few, the boxing he'd taken as part of his phys ed at school coming in handy.

It felt good. Hitting. Over and over. Finally being the one inflicting pain.

It was only as he realized he kneeled over the man about to hit his already bloody face that he paused.

This wasn't him.

Rok shoved off his dad and headed for the bathroom to rinse his knuckles.

"Weak," his father warbled, having tottered to the door.

"Weak because I don't want you dead?"

"You are not my son."

"You've made that clear."

"Then why do you stay?"

Why did he stay? It would take only a minute to stuff a bag.

His father shifted to block his exit from the bathroom.

"Move."

"Make me." Samuel sneered.

"Do you want me to kill you?"

"We both know you won't. Which will be your downfall."

"Is there a point to this conversation?"

"You will never be Alpha. You're soft."

"Who says I want to be alpha? Not everyone wants to rule."

"You say that now, but if I were to wait five, ten

years, you'll be eyeing my spot and thinking you can take over simply because I squirted inside your mother."

"Keep your pack. If I want one, I'll make my own."

His father laughed. "As if they'd give a weakling like you anything."

"Maybe with me gone you'll stop being so bitter," was the last thing Rok said to his dad.

As for Samuel, he shouted, "Stupid fucker. So smug and righteous about leaving me alive. Know that, one day, I will find you. And when I do, you'll die."

It seemed the reckoning had finally arrived. The problem being now Rok had something to lose.

Meadow.

Despite the rain, he caught her scent the moment he hit the path to the forest. How far behind was he? He had no sense of time as to how long ago she'd left. He ran, half dressed and panicked. The need to change pulsed, but he didn't want to scare Meadow either.

He almost shredded everything when he heard her scream.

He was close now. Close enough he could hear the creek rushing. The scuffs of a fight. The woods thinned, and he saw Meadow facing off against

Samuel. Worse, he could see past them to the coming tidal wave.

Rok couldn't reach Meadow in time. The raging creek took her while the man responsible stood watching from the shore.

With a roar, Amarok ran, but not for Samuel. That man didn't deserve his attention. He raced parallel to the raging storm water, trying to keep an eye on Meadow, who bobbed in the torrent.

My fault.

The deluge spilled into a makeshift lake, the current splitting and spreading. She grabbed hold of a tree, arms and legs wrapped tight, facing away from him.

Rok spared a glance behind. He didn't see his father, but that didn't mean he hadn't followed. He took a step into the water before letting her know he'd arrived. "I'm here, Doe. Hold on."

"Rok!" She squealed his name. "Your dad is here. He's crazy."

"I know. Forget about him. Let's get you somewhere safe."

She inched around her tree until she could see him. Her smile shouldn't have been so bright at the sight of him. "You're able to walk. Is it deep?"

"Deep enough where you are so don't let go." He didn't want her losing her footing.

"I think I should have stayed in bed."

"I think you might be right."

Her nose wrinkled. "Your dad needs serious help."

"He needs to die and stop making people miserable," was his muttered reply.

"What did you say?"

"That you were supposed to take it easy."

"It was just a little walk. And then a tidal wave got me."

The closer to her he waded, the more the current tugged at his legs.

"Sorry about your dad."

"Told you he was a dick."

She managed a half-laugh. Then a scream. "Behind you!"

He whirled and ducked. The branch his father threw like a javelin soared past.

Rok snapped, "Fuck off. Haven't you done enough?"

"It will never be enough. You took away the one thing I loved. So now it's my turn to take yours."

His father glanced past him to Meadow, picked up a stone from the shore, and threw. It just missed. He grabbed another.

"Fucker!" Rok lost his shit. With a roar more

beast than man, he charged, splashing out of the water.

His father met him with a swing. Rok ducked. Punched.

They slugged it out, meaty thuds that sprayed rain, blood, and spit. But now, as then, Rok was stronger. Faster.

His father fell to the ground.

Rok could end this. Right here. Right now.

"Go ahead. Do it," his father taunted. "Kill me like you killed your mother."

"I don't need to. You're already dead to me." He turned away to see Meadow had chosen to try and wade to shore, her movements slow as she struggled with the current.

Behind him, Samuel muttered a contempt-laced, "Weak."

Rok flashed him the finger over his shoulder. "Keep walking, Doe. I'm coming."

She shot him a tremulous smile as she slogged. An expression that turned to horror as she looked past him.

Damn his father for not conceding. He turned, expecting to see the man. A mistake.

The wolf hit him hard, a hundred and eighty pounds of pissed-off fur, teeth, and claws. They slammed into the ground, but Rok fought through the disorientation and braced his arm against the wolf's lower jaw, keeping the snapping teeth from his face.

What had Samuel done? He'd shifted in front of Meadow. If anyone were to find out...

And they would if Samuel escaped. He'd tell everyone about the human who knew their secret. Given she wasn't mated to someone in a pack and bound by oath, she'd be dead within a day.

Samuel had to die.

The problem being, as a wolf, Samuel now had the advantage, leaving Rok no choice. He'd explain to Meadow later.

He rammed his knees between their bodies and shoved the gray wolf from his chest. Standing, he had only a moment to shout, "Don't be afraid," before the shift took him.

He no longer screamed with the agony that came with the first time. He exploded into white fur, a gift from his mother, and a mean attitude that got meaner as his mate's fear scent drifted to him.

He'd tend to her as soon as he removed the threat. The gray wolf bared his teeth and growled.

Come on then. My bite is bigger.

They met in a clash of fur, claws, and teeth. Snapping. Chomping. Wrestling, trying to get the advantage knowing whoever got hold of a neck first would win.

It all depended on who tired first. Who would fuck up.

Not Rok.

He got his father's throat in his teeth and squeezed. Samuel's breath rattled and rolled.

A little more pressure and the nightmare would be over. He'd never have to worry about Daddy coming to give him a lesson on respect anymore.

Father killer.

He let go and backed away, shifting back to man. Naked, and covered in his and his father's blood.

A whimper turned his head.

A wide terrified gaze met his. *My mate fears.*

Not liking that, he growled, which was the wrong thing to do.

She moaned. "No. No. No."

But what killed him was when she bolted in fear. With the wolf still simmering in his blood, he couldn't help but take off after her.

TWENTY-TWO

HE'S A WOLF.

The thought panted in Meadow's head, along with the replay of what happened. First the gray wolf came out of nowhere to pounce Rok, its mouth wide with a slavering snarl. Then Rok wasn't himself. He turned into a big freaking white wolf.

Werewolf. Had to be. And the gray one that attacked him? His dad. Inherited? Or a virus like movies and books claimed?

Panic hit. How contagious was it?

Oh god. He'd kissed her. They'd swapped spit a few times now. Would she be a werewolf, too? Please, no, she already hated shaving her legs every few days. She could only imagine being a werewolf would be worse.

As she bolted, breath heaving, she tried to focus on anything but the beast possibly chasing her. Thought about how that morning for breakfast she didn't crave more meat than usual. Guess she'd know for sure if she howled at the next full moon.

Branches whipped past her face, snagging hair and sopping clothes. She'd lost a boot in the tidal wave and clomped. *Squish. Clomp. Squish.*

"Doe, stop." Rok's plea came to her, and she almost stopped. If this were a movie, what would she be yelling at the screen?

Run.

Rok might be a good guy, but his dad was a psycho. The things he'd said. The way he'd attacked. Wasn't insanity hereditary?

And who cared really about their mental state? The fight itself had been savage. Terrifying. Two wild animals tearing at each other. What if Rok turned on her? She'd be mauled in mere seconds.

"Please don't be scared. I would never hurt you."

The claim, heard amidst her panting panic, caused her to pause. Especially since it sounded close. A glance over her shoulder showed him jogging at her naked.

Dick and balls bouncing, incongruous enough she laughed. Hysterically. It didn't help he scowled as he stood in front of her, hands on his hips. Hanging out.

She laughed harder.

"What's so funny?"

"Men shouldn't run without bottoms," she tried to explain between snickers and hiccups for air.

He took offense. "It's cold outside."

Her lips curved. "Wasn't talking about size but jiggle."

"Oh. In that case, you might have a point." He offered a sheepish grin.

For a second, it occurred how normal he seemed. Then she remembered.

"You're a werewolf!" She took a step back.

"Yes."

He didn't even try and deny it. "Am I infected?"

"What? No. Of course not."

"Says you."

"Yes, says me," he huffed. "It's not a fucking disease. We're born this way."

She cocked her head. "No. It's not possible. The genetics alone say it wouldn't work."

"And yet here I am."

He was. In the naked flesh, making it harder to remind herself of the beast within.

"What happened to your father? Did you kill him?" Because she knew he came close. Wouldn't have blamed him. Some evils shouldn't breathe the same air the rest of the world did.

"Fucker's still bitching and moaning."

"He's unstable."

"No shit. He'll have to be dealt with. Just not by me."

"That's probably a good idea."

"You must be cold."

"A little." She shivered.

"Come on. I know a place nearby we can warm up before heading back."

"Why not go back now?"

"Because I don't know if I'm ready for people yet. You?"

Only one person she really wanted to see, and he was with her. Still... "Won't your friends worry? And what about your dad?"

"Darian's already handling Samuel and knows I came after you."

"Is Darian..." She couldn't say it out loud.

"I'm not doing answers while freezing my dick off."

She wasn't feeling too warm herself in her wet clothes. "Show me your secret hideout."

The shelter in question proved to be literally less than a minute away. Camo netting covered the opening of a cave, keeping it dry. He lit a lantern to chase the gloom before he ignited a little propane heater that, despite being in the opening, quickly exuded warmth. He shook out a blanket tucked in a naturally formed alcove.

"What is this place?"

"Hunting blind for goose season."

Looking around, she saw no signs of blood or bones. "You hunt?"

"Not me. And you can stop looking nervous. I didn't bring you here to murder you."

Her eyes widened. It hadn't even occurred to her dumb butt until he said it. "Why are we here?"

"Because I wanted some time alone with you before we had to deal with everyone."

"Can't blame you for wanting to avoid dealing with your dad." Her nose wrinkled.

"With any luck, I won't have to."

"What's going to happen to him?"

"He'll be severely punished for his actions."

"By who? You?"

He shook his head. "Someone else will handle it."

"You don't mean the cops, do you?"

"Not even close." He scrubbed a hand through his wet hair. "Let's just say Weres have their own judicial system."

"Implying there are many more than just you

and your dad." Her mind spun to the people she'd recently met. "Is everyone at the ranch like you?" Had she been the lamb eating with the wolves this entire time?

"Yes, which is why you can't say anything." He tilted her chin. "This is the biggest secret you'll ever know. Meaning it's important you never tell anyone what you saw and what I'm telling you right now."

She sat on a rock that made a perfect stool, while he leaned against a cave wall. "As if anyone would believe me."

"Even in jest. You must never ever say anything about what you saw my father or me do."

"Or what?"

"Things will go badly for all of us."

She bit her lip and almost laughed at the melodramatic statement, only Rok didn't seem to be one prone to exaggerations. If he said zip it or else, she should pay attention.

"I won't say a word." But she might indulge in a bit of an inner scream fest. Werewolves existed. This was huge. Exciting. Especially since he didn't seem inclined to eat her.

"I mean it, Meadow. The humans can't ever know about us."

She might have thought him melodramatic, but

then again, she'd seen what happened to rare animals. Captured. Studied. Caged.

"You won't have to worry about me. I solemnly swear to never divulge your secret to another human being," she vowed and crossed her heart.

His eyes turned into amber mirrors for a second, as if they reflected the lantern light. "Good."

"I guess werewolf club is like fight club. The first rule is there is no club."

"What?" He blinked at her.

"Come on, you have to know that movie. You live in the boonies. What else do you have to do?"

He grinned. "Just fucking with you. You're right. The first rule is deny, deny, deny."

"I'll deny it, but I have to ask, why hide your existence?"

He arched a brow. "I'd say it's obvious. The world isn't ready for us."

"Don't be so sure. People are getting better about individual differences. Hair color. Skin. Beliefs."

He arched a brow. "Werewolves might be stretching the diversity factor."

"So you hide in the woods. Seems kind of lonely."

"Only if you enjoy crowds. Which I don't. And don't think my situation is the norm. Many Weres live urban and suburban lives."

"And nobody knows?"

He shook his head.

"Damn." The realization turned her pensive. It was a bit shattering to realize the world held more secrets than expected.

He moved closer and crouched before her. "I'm sorry I broke you."

She frowned. "What are you talking about?"

"You lost your smile." His hand reached out to run a finger over her lower lip.

She almost nipped it. "Blame your dad for that. You didn't do anything."

He cupped her face. "I should have been there to protect you."

"Pretty sure no one predicted crazy daddy attacking in the woods as a possibility if I went for a walk."

"You should have stayed in bed."

"I couldn't. I needed air." She ducked her head.

"Implying you were upset before my dad." His turn for his brow to furrow. "Why?"

"I thought it was my fault your friend died."

"Wallace? He was killed by Samuel."

"Your dad murdered him!" She shivered, realizing anew how close she'd come to death herself.

"You're cold. Let's get you out of the wet stuff."

He barely touched her as he helped her strip,

taking her clothes and doing his best to hang them on knobby protrusions.

The field blanket, while good at repelling moisture, did not have comfort in mind. Still, she huddled under it as he aimed the little heater at her.

It quickly warmed her shivering frame, or was it him sitting close to her, his arm around her shoulders, tucking her into his body? The man exuded heat but very little conversation.

She couldn't stand the silence. "Sorry I bolted. The whole wolf thing took me by surprise."

"Kind of understandable."

"What would you have done if I hadn't stopped running?" she asked.

"Tackled you."

"What?" She shoved at him in surprise. "You're not supposed to hit girls."

"That's sexist and offensive. But if it helps, I would never hurt you. I would have made sure you landed on top."

"You claim you won't hurt me, but how can I tell if that's the truth?"

"You can't."

She glanced at him. "Not even going to try and convince me?"

"Not much point. Either you trust me or you don't."

"Depends, got any more secrets?"

"None as big as being a Were, unless you count a secret love for Britney Spears songs."

That got her giggling. "That I have to see to believe."

"If you're lucky, maybe I'll serenade you."

She outright laughed. "No way. I don't believe it." She wrinkled her nose. "Then again, a day ago I wouldn't have believed you were a werewolf. Have you always been one?"

"Since birth, but I didn't shift until my hormones started raging in my preteens. Most of my kind start being able to change into their wolf around eleven or twelve. I was a late bloomer at almost fifteen. My mother was a no-shower. Someone who had Were parents but can't shift themselves."

"Are there many of you?"

His lips pressed into a line. "I should stop talking about it until you understand a few things."

"Or we don't talk at all." She leaned into him. Then she broke her own suggestion saying, "You swear I won't turn into a werewolf from being close to you?"

"No."

"Even if we're like really close?" she hinted.

"I could give you a blood transfusion and you'd still not be any furrier."

Reassuring even as something occurred to her. "You're trusting me quite a bit by telling me this, aren't you?"

"Yup."

"Why? You barely know me, and this is a big deal. You said it yourself, no one is supposed to know."

"Kind of hard to not say anything given what you saw. And I've seen enough of you to gauge you're a good person. You'd never intentionally fuck anyone over."

An accurate assessment. "Thank you." Then on impulse, she kissed him. A light brush of her lips.

He sucked in a breath. "You shouldn't do that."

"Why?"

"Because it might lead to us doing other things, and I don't have a condom handy."

A man who played safe. "Would it help if I said I've been checked since my last, um, encounter?" She blushed and looked at her bare toes. Dirty toes.

"I'm clean as well. But I don't want to risk a baby."

"So only a condom works?" Probably one of the frankest conversations of her life and the most heated. Her cheeks might never need blush again. "Because I'm on the pill." Would it work against his swimmers? Contemplating sex with a werewolf was one thing; puppies was another.

"Pill, IUD, all the usual methods work." A gruff reply.

Good. But she still had questions. "You won't bite me?"

"Only if you want me to," he teased.

"I'd rather you kissed me."

TWENTY-THREE

Rok wanted to kiss Meadow. Intense relief filled him at the realization she hadn't been injured and that she'd gotten over her initial fear at discovering his wolf side.

He could smell her arousal. She wanted him. And he wanted her something fierce. But before he could embrace her, they needed to further discuss the Were secret.

The moment Samuel shifted he'd condemned her. There were only a few outcomes in this situation.

One, no one found out. Which would involve Samuel keeping his yapper shut, Darian not having seen anything involving Meadow, and Meadow herself never ever saying a word once she left.

Don't like that option. Mostly the Meadow-leaving aspect.

Which left only two other choices. One of those being death.

The last option terrified Rok because, in it, he claimed her as his mate then hunted down an Alpha to accept her pledge. But he had limited time to do one without the other. Humans who knew the secret had to be oathbound, quickly, or die.

The Lykosium wouldn't be overt about it. The accident would never cause suspicion, but it would happen, even to those who thought no one had found out. The Lykosium always knew.

The human had an accident, and their Were mate, who'd failed to follow the rules, might serve an example as well. The Lykosium took no chances with their secret.

If only Meadow's promise to him could count. He could smell the truth when she swore she'd never tell, but only a binding oath given to an Alpha would do. It held a magic no one understood that forced a promise to be kept.

"You're so serious." Her gaze met his. "You don't have to kiss me."

"I want to. It's just a little more complicated for my kind."

"Because I'm human." Her nose wrinkled.

"Because you're my mate." The truth slipped out, and he didn't take it back.

She blinked. "What kind of mate are we talking about? The friendly kind or the other?"

"What if I said you're mine and I've known it since we met?"

She laughed. "I'd say you don't need to make up stuff to get frisky with me."

"It's true. I know my actions haven't necessarily reflected it, but that's only because I'm still struggling with the idea. You're mine. My mate." The more he said it, the more concrete it felt. Right.

Her mouth rounded. "I don't know what to say."

"Say you'll be mine."

"Just like that? After only a few days?"

"Tell me you don't feel it."

"I feel it. It's wild and crazy and—"

"Right."

"Yes, right." She cupped his cheek. "It's like something in a story."

"It's exactly how it should be when mates meet."

"And what happens once they do?" she asked. She was on her knees between his legs, her mouth tilted toward his.

"The attraction is instant."

"And well hidden by grumpiness," she teased, the words hot over his lips.

"I don't want to hide it anymore." His fingers spanned the back of her neck. "Then they kiss and claim each other."

"Just like that?"

"If they're mates, there's no stopping it."

"So if we have sex, I could end up your mate?"

"Not could, will."

"For how long?"

"Forever."

"Okay." She imprinted the word on his mouth as she embraced him. Her hands skimmed his body. He returned the favor. There were no clothes to impede her discovery. No interruptions. Nothing but him and her.

The blanket covered the ground, the heater kept them warm, but he made sure she was even warmer. He partially covered her, one leg inserted between her thighs, pushing against her heated core.

He palmed a breast, squeezing the fullness, ready to suck. But that would require relinquishing her mouth, and it tasted too sweet.

She panted against his lips. Her tongue slid sinuously against his. She held him by the hair, hungry for his kiss.

Her entire body undulated against him, needing more than kisses and simple touch. He dragged his mouth across the fine line of her jaw and down her neck, nipping her skin, sucking it in spots. He straddled her that he might cup her breasts and push them together, a feast for his mouth. He sucked those pebbled tips. Flicked them with his tongue. Played with her breasts until she moaned, "More."

Her hips rolled, inviting him to move lower. He settled himself between her legs, the scent of her driving him wild. He needed her.

Would have her.

But first, she would come for him.

He licked her. And she moaned.

He swirled his tongue over her again, splitting apart her nether lips, finding her pleasure spot. She writhed.

He teased her with his lips and tongue, holding her aloft that he might feast on her until her body clenched and she cried out his name.

"Rok!"

Her orgasm still rolling through her body, he rose above her and growled, "Doe, look at me."

Passion-glazed eyes met his. The tip of his cock tickled the entrance to her sex. Wet. Pulsing.

Her lips parted, and she purred, "Mine."

Oh, there was no resisting that. He slammed into her, and she cried out in pleasure and clung to him with her nails. He thrust her into another climax and kept pounding, drawing it out until she clawed at him and screamed so loud it came out silent.

He reached the pinnacle just a second after her. His body arched. His dick pulsed and expanded, as he didn't just come.

He marked her as his. He felt it the moment the claiming happened. As if everything inside him tilted and became something more.

Within days, her scent would change, and all would notice. Know they belonged together. It also meant the clock had started when it came to getting her oathbound. Once he had her pledged, no one would be able to take her away.

"Mine," he murmured as he rolled over her and drew her close.

"I like the sound of that," she murmured against his chest.

"We'll have to go on a road trip soon as we get back to the ranch."

"Where are we going?"

"Remember how you promised me you'd never say anything to anyone?"

"Yeah."

"We kind of have to make it official."

"With who?" She leaned up on his chest, her hair a silken fall that framed her face.

"Someone that counts. You'll swear an oath to never say anything and all will be good."

"That doesn't sound so bad."

"It's an oath that can never be broken or—"

Her stomach took that moment to utter a profound growl of hunger.

"You need food."

"I can wait. I want to hear more about you. It's nice that you're talking to me."

He plucked the hand that cupped his cheek and kissed the fingers. "And we will talk plenty over some food in warm clothing. I'll bet Poppy's baked a feast by now."

"I'd do anything for her hot cocoa." She practically moaned it. In her defense, it was pretty damned good.

It was clothing to trudge home that proved a dilemma. Hers was cold and wet, while he had none. He could go in fur, but that might be pushing things. Thus far, no one knew she'd seen a Were.

"We'll go naked. It's not a big deal," he tried to convince her. "It's just skin. We've all seen it."

She shook her head. "I can't. I use cubicles when changing at the gym. Guess I'm pulling on wet clothes." She shuddered in distaste.

"No, you're not. I'll pop back to the house and get a bag of dry stuff. We're not that far. If I run there and back, I'll be like forty minutes. Forty-two tops if I get waylaid by anyone."

"If it's any longer, then you better have a Thermos along with my shoes."

He laughed. "Deal. Wait for me. Don't go anywhere."

"I don't think that will be a problem," was her dry reply.

And yet she wasn't there when he returned.

TWENTY-FOUR

IN THE MINUTES AFTER ROK LEFT, MEADOW LAY on the rough blanket and basked by the heater. Her body had never felt more relaxed. Sated.

As a lover, Rok exceeded all expectation and experience. Said all the rights things.

Then left her in a cave.

As the seconds ticked by and the glow receded, it occurred to her she was alone with no idea where she was in context to the ranch. Not far, obviously, but what direction? Getting lost out here? Super bad idea. People died making the wrong turn in the woods.

Stop panicking. After all the things Rok said, he'd return. He'd told her he'd need a few minutes to get back to the house. Pack a bag. Come back.

He wouldn't just abandon her in this hole, right?

Meadow knew what Valencia would say, *"You're too trusting."* Not inaccurate. Meadow preferred to believe people were ultimately good, in direct contrast to her best friend. Val trusted hardly anyone. Meadow being one of a few. Meadow's parents, though, didn't make the cut. According to Val, *"They'd sell me out in a second to save you. Don't even deny it."*

Meadow wasn't so sure. Her parents adored Val and treated her like another daughter. As for Val, while she would gruffly deny it, she'd have died for Mom and Dad. Her friend had a bigger heart than she liked to admit. What would she think of Rok? She definitely wouldn't approve of Meadow lying around naked, waiting for a man to save her.

She sat up on her blanket and stared at the covering over the cave. The netting was thick enough to block view except for the corner folded back for the heater to sit and spew its fumes. She wouldn't suffocate or die of carbon monoxide poisoning. Maybe.

Perhaps a few heaves of fresh air would be a good idea. She crept for the opening, conscious it was day outside. Pouring rain, but still bright enough someone could see her.

Exactly *who* would see her?

Meadow grabbed the netting, about to pull it

back when someone called to her. "Meadow. Meadow Fields, are you nearby? Can you hear me?"

Yes, and yes. She glanced at her naked body. Oh dear. Panic set in. She needed clothes. The wet, sopping mess wouldn't be fun to put on at all. That left the blanket, which she realized had a wet spot. Lovely. Her second choice was lubed in sex juice. Dammit.

"Ms. Fields, if you can hear me, answer. I know you're nearby."

Who was it? She didn't recognize their voice, and how did they know she was here?

Shit. Could he see the light from the battery-operated lantern? She glanced behind at it. It didn't seem that bright. Was it enough to outline her?

Please don't tell me I was playing shadow puppet.

"I'm coming in."

Her eyes widened. "No. You can't," she blurted out.

"Are you being threatened, Ms. Fields?"

"What? No, I'm fine. Just a little underdressed. Due to the rain and my clothes being wet, so Rok took them off. I mean I did after he said he'd get me some dry stuff."

"I have dry clothing you can have."

"Really?" Suspicion set in. "Hold on a second.

You were looking for me. How did you know I was here? Did Rok send you?"

"Not exactly."

"Then how did you know where to find me?"

"I tracked you."

"This place isn't exactly easy to find."

She peeked around the camo curtain, searching for the voice. He stood downhill a bit, wearing a poncho, its hood drawn low over his brow. He held up a knapsack.

It had to hold the aforementioned clothes. She could practically feel them covering her skin. Naked was nice in a bedroom, with the door locked where no one could interrupt. Right now, she felt very disadvantaged.

"How do I know you're not some crazy guy?"

"Would it help if I said I know everything there is to know about this ranch? I can name everyone if you'd like. Give you personal details."

"What's Astra's stance on marshmallows topping cocoa?" she asked.

"Poppy is the one who cooks, and she doesn't add anything to it."

Her tension eased a bit. "How come we haven't met?"

"Hasn't been a chance before now. You may call

me Kit. Where would you like this?" He jiggled the bag.

"Do you make it a habit of wandering around the woods, carrying clothes to give to women?"

"I told you I tracked you. Did you think I'd come here unprepared?" He tossed the bag, and it hit the lip in front of the shallow cave.

"You keep saying tracked. How?"

"As if you don't know."

She didn't but wondered if it was a wolf thing. Was this Kit another one? She couldn't see the man's features. The hood remained pulled low, and the poncho hid his shape. His presence made her uncomfortable, but at the same time, there wasn't much she could do to rid herself of him. Might as well see what he offered.

She snared the bag and pulled it open to find a dark gray tracksuit, a bit large but warm. The shoes were rubberized pull-ons, also a bit big, but they covered her feet.

He talked as she dressed. "One has to wonder why the choice to come here rather than return to the ranch where you could have immediately changed into dry clothes."

How to explain Rok wanted time alone with her to deal with what she'd seen? She made something up before pulling back the tarp. "He thought I'd like it. It's very, um, peaceful to listen to the rain."

The man remained at the bottom of the incline. "It's just surprising, what with his father being here, challenging him."

"You know about his father?" She made her way down the slope, the rain holding off slightly but the descent slippery.

"I'm here because of Samuel. I hear you had an encounter with him."

"We did." She hedged, conscious of the promise she'd made Rok.

"It's okay. You can speak to me. I know about the wolf attack."

She exhaled. "So you know everything."

"Not entirely. Just that you saw Samuel change into a wolf and Amarok also shifted to protect you."

Meadow grimaced. "It was terrifying."

"I take it you didn't know Amarok could shift?" the man asked, handing her a poncho still creased from its packaging.

"No. I'm still trying to process it now." She was also wondering at this interrogation-style rescue. "Who sent you to find me?" Because she began to wonder if it wasn't Rok after all.

Rather than reply to her query, he tossed a new

one of his own. "How many other times have you seen Amarok's wolf?"

The question took her by surprise. Flustered, she said, "Just the one time."

"Are you sure?"

"It's not something I could forget," she snapped. "His dad turned into a big gray, and I thought he was going to eat Rok. But then Rok was this even bigger white wolf and they were snarling at each other. It was terrifying. Lucky for me, Rok won."

"He killed his father?"

"No. He walked away. It's why we came here. He needed a bit of time to decompress."

"And is this when he explained to you about Weres, or were you already aware of them?"

"Just found out. Talk about wild. Are you a wolf, too?" she asked, still unable to see more than the jaw of Kit's face.

Again, he avoided her question. "How much do you know about the Were?"

"Just the basics. Werewolves are real. Born, not made. And not contagious. Which was a relief." She blushed as she suddenly realized how he probably construed it.

He veered in a different direction. "Did you give oath?"

"Excuse me."

"It is a simple question. Did you swear an oath?"

"You mean promise not to tell any secrets? Yeah, I told Rok I would never say anything. Mum's the word." She pulled a zipper over her lips.

"You promised him, no one else?"

"Why does it matter? I'm not going to tell." Only technically she just had to this man who'd managed to trick her into spilling everything.

"Did he mate you?"

"I don't see that as being any of your business," she huffed.

"Guess we'll know in a few days if the scent takes," Kit muttered.

"Excuse me, what scent? What are you talking about?"

"Apparently you're not as well informed as you think. Come with me. All will be explained."

'I'd rather not." It was one thing to converse and take the clothes Kit offered, another to trust this stranger and go off with him. "I'll wait for Rok."

"You will come using your two feet, or I will knock you out and carry you. Which, I will add, is not my preference, as it is more work for me."

"You'd hit a girl?"

"Yes, because I'm not sexist."

Her mouth rounded. "Who are you? You don't work on the ranch, do you?"

"Nope. And I am not someone you can ignore. Let's go."

"Go where?"

He sighed. "Why must everyone ask that?" His hands lifted to push back his hood, revealing flame-red hair and an uncanny gaze.

In the distance, she heard a howl.

Kit cocked his head. "We need to go now."

Never go willingly. That was the advice in her self-defense class. She bolted.

He sighed. "Why must they always run?"

Meadow didn't make it more than three steps before Kit caught her. He snared her wrists, tie-wrapped them, and then tossed her over his shoulder.

Casual like.

As if he'd done this before.

Eep.

"Rok will find me," she stated with assurance.

"He'll try. Unfortunately, he won't arrive in time."

"Is this some kind of vendetta?"

"Hardly. I don't make the laws. I simply gather evidence of those breaking them, and in this case, there's plenty."

"Evidence of what? His father attacked me and Rok. Roc's not guilty of anything."

"By your own admission, you are not oathbound. And yet the one known as Amarok Fleetfoot revealed our existence."

"By accident. He would have been killed otherwise," she added.

"Our rules are clear. Only oathbound humans can know about the Were."

"I told you, I already promised Rok I wouldn't tell anyone."

"And yet immediately spoke to me about it."

"Because you obviously knew already," she exclaimed in exasperation.

"What if I were simply laying a verbal trap? This is why the Oath is needed."

"And I was going to give it. Rok said we'd go somewhere and get one done."

"Rok should have secured your Oath before telling you anything."

"Could you be any more paranoid? No one is out to get you," she declared with a roll of her eyes, which he didn't get to appreciate.

"The rules exist for a reason. You broke them and now must face the consequences."

"You can't be serious."

"Very serious. Your Amarok is in much trouble. As are you." He said it without inflection, his stride steady.

"We've done nothing wrong."

"That is not up to me to judge."

"Who then?"

"You will meet them when I present my report about Amarok's activities. You are evidence of his crime."

Her mouth opened and shut. "I won't testify."

"You won't have a choice."

"Like hell I don't."

Kit went on as if she didn't have a say. "You will be detained until a decision is reached."

"A decision about what?" she exclaimed, twisting in his grip to no avail. She'd not heard any more howling.

"A decision on whether you live or die."

"That's a bit dramatic." She used sarcasm to counter fear. It wasn't working. A chill filled her, making her realize she'd stepped into something serious and deadly.

"Welcome to Were World."

"That's a brilliant name. WWW. Everyone will assume the merchandise glorifies the internet."

"Are you insane?"

"No."

"Shame. It might have reduced your sentence."

"What's less than death?"

"There are shades of death. Long and drawn out. Quick. Painless."

He listed off a few more, enough for her to sputter, "You're the crazy one. Kidnapping women. Threatening to kill them."

"Would it help if I said I get bonuses if you require being subdued?"

She quieted, but only so she could simmer and plot. Nothing great because, even now, violence didn't come naturally to her.

His steps brought them to a clear track, the wheel ruts full of water. A massive truck, its paint scratched and rusting, sat beside a stack of felled trees.

If she'd wondered how Kit planned to smuggle her out past Rok, she'd just got her answer. Kit was using the logging trails.

He tossed her into the passenger seat and slammed the door shut. As he headed around to the driver's side, she threw open the door and fell out. Immediately she struggled to her feet and took a step, digging her toes in to sprint.

This time, Kit didn't just tackle her. The needle he jabbed her with knocked her out.

TWENTY-FIVE

Filled with a sense of urgency, Rok raced back to the cave. It wasn't fast enough. He'd barely been gone, and yet she'd disappeared.

The heater still burned propane. The covered cave was warm. No sign of Meadow. Just the scent of her on the blanket left behind, along with her sopping clothes. She wouldn't have left without anything.

This was bad.

He ran back outside. "Doe! Where are you?"

The moisture, hanging heavy in the air, distorted all scent. Tracking downward from the cave, he located an empty knapsack. A strange aroma clung to the fibers, mostly artificial pinecone. Some fox. And something that reminded him of Were. He couldn't help but think of that picture of an animal that shouldn't exist.

Just how many goddamned people were running around his forest?

As if he didn't already have enough to deal with. For fuck's sake, the moment he'd walked into his house it was to find everyone in an uproar.

"Where have you been?" Darian yelled as Rok stepped into the kitchen, still tying the sash on the robe he'd snared.

"What's wrong?" After the bout in the hunting blind with Meadow, Rok was feeling mellow.

"Your dad, that's what," Hammer announced.

Oh fuck, there went his glow. "What about Samuel? Don't tell me you lost him." Darian had taken over before he bolted after Meadow.

"We didn't lose him, although I wanted to strangle him," Darian grimly proclaimed. "He's a nasty piece of work."

"Understatement." Nova pushed off the counter and gestured with her hands. "Thought me mum was bad, but Jeezus, that man is foul."

"He ranted the entire time we dragged his ass back to the house." Hammer continued the narrative.

"Until Lochlan told him to shut up. When he didn't, Lochlan planted one on his kisser." Asher slammed his fist into his open palm.

Speaking of... "Where is Lochlan?" He wasn't in the room.

"Says we're too loud for him. He went to his cabin."

"Where's my dad—Samuel— now?"

"Gone."

"What do you mean he's gone? You said you didn't lose him!" he exploded. "Why aren't you out there tracking him down? The man is fucking dangerous."

"No shit. Explains why a Lykosium squad of enforcers arrived and took him into custody."

Rok froze at the words. "What the fuck did you just say?"

Darian repeated it more slowly, "There were Lykosium soldiers waiting for us at the house. Three massive SUVs, a couple people in each. Two standing watch on the porch. Soon as they heard us coming, they announced their presence. Informed us we were told to hand over one Samuel Fleetfoot immediately for judgment by the Lykosium."

The Lykosium being those who governed the Were. Protected their secrets. Settled disputes. Kept them in line.

"So they finally arrested him. Just a few decades too late." A bitter chuckle. "Any idea where they took Samuel?"

"They didn't say," Darian offered with a shrug.

"Because it's Lykosium business now." Given how many rules Samuel had broken, he'd probably die. The Lykosium wouldn't tolerate anyone upsetting their secrets. "At least it's out of my hands then."

Everyone looked at each other, but it was Nova who said it out loud. "Your father didn't go quietly. He told them that Meadow knows about us."

"Fucking Samuel." The shitty gift that kept on giving.

"So it's true?" Darian asked. "She knows?"

"Only because that dick shifted right in front of her. He did it on purpose."

"I don't know if the soldiers believed him, because they told him to shut his mouth, and when he wouldn't, they gagged him."

"Good." But only until they questioned him again and Samuel did his best to fuck Rok over.

"Where is Meadow?" Nova asked. "She didn't come back with you."

"She was cold and wet, so I took her to the goose blind to warm up."

"Just warm up?" Nova arched a brow, and Rok almost blushed.

"Fuck his sex life, we have bigger problems if Meadow knows," Darian pointed out.

"Don't shit a brick. It's okay. We talked. She won't tell."

"She's not oathbound," Darian stressed.

"She will be, soon as I can manage it. I just came to grab some dry clothes for me and her. We'll drive tonight for Calgary. There's an Alpha there that might be willing to hear her pledge if I offer him a discount on fresh meat. Everything will be okay."

It didn't ease their worry. He even understood their fear. Would the Lykosium enforcers return to condemn Meadow for knowing their secret? Would Rok and the others be considered accomplices, an almost greater crime?

"She needs to be oathbound ASAP. Bad enough the Lykosium noticed we were out here. If they think we're causing trouble..." Bellamy was worried. And rightly so with his wife close to giving birth.

Lone wolves didn't have the protection of a pack. The Lykosium was the one to rule them where the laws were concerned. And they could be strict.

Knowing his father would sing louder than a canary, Rok had dressed quickly and grabbed a bag that appeared to have clothes for Meadow. Given speed trumped noise, he took an ATV back to the cave.

Only he arrived too late. The cave was empty,

and he could only assume somehow the Lykosium enforcers got to her first.

But how?

No one knew about this place but Rok and the others at the ranch. And even then, only Hammer and Lochlan ever used it much.

Someone watching them, though, would have possibly found it. That would imply the Lykosium were spying on them for a while. He thought of the various signs they'd found of someone trespassing.

While Samuel watched them, had someone else been spying on Samuel?

If yes, then they might all be in trouble. He should get back and warn the others. His phone had no signal this deep in the woods. He glanced away from the cave. Someone wanting to avoid the ranch might have taken the logging trails.

He glanced back at the ranch. If they were screwed, an hour wouldn't make a difference.

But it might save Meadow.

He jumped on the ATV and gunned it, ripping through the trees, choosing speed over stealth. He knew exactly where the logging road ended. The ATV flew out of the forest, all four wheels in the air as a hump launched him. It was only enough to see taillights disappearing in the distance.

Too late.

He wasted a few kilometers trying to catch them before admitting defeat. The trek home was at a slower pace as he tried to absorb the fact he'd failed. How would he find Meadow?

If the Lykosium took her, would they execute her right away? They'd better not. He deserved a chance to argue his case. Yes, he'd broken rules, but the circumstances should accord him some leeway.

Fucking Samuel. He'd mucked things up royally. Perhaps Rok could contact the Lykosium and make it clear only he was to blame.

Would they listen, though?

He arrived home to find grim expressions. Hadn't there been enough shit news for one day? He raked fingers through his damp hair. "Now what?"

"We found this at the door."

It was a box, wooden and plain. A simple hasp held it shut, and a crescent moon was carved crookedly on its lid. A deceptively mundane cover for what it held.

This benign-looking box, small enough to sit in the palm of his hand, was from the Lykosium. It meant it was keyed to only open for the right person. Any attempts to pry it open would destroy it.

His stomach bottomed out. "I assume you've all had a chance to hold it?"

They nodded.

Rok had never received one before, but his uncle had. About six months after Rok's arrival on the ranch. Uncle Tomas left and was gone for ten days. When he came back to the ranch, Uncle never spoke of it again. Rok didn't push it and counted himself lucky. According to rumor, not everyone who was summoned returned.

The box dared him to touch.

He didn't want to.

But he had to.

He noticed all his friends held their breaths as he took the box in his hand. He pressed the pad of his thumb against the clasp.

A zing of electricity jolted. The clasp made no sound as it disappeared. The lid opened as if on a hydraulic hinge, slowly revealing the simple interior that held only a note, the calligraphy impressive.

Amarok Fleetfoot is to present himself to the Lykosium Council on the third day after receiving this missive. Failure to appear will have conse-quences. And then an address in Bulgaria.

He had barely enough time to be sure he memo-rized it before the note and box turned to ash, until only a fine silt remained.

"What did it say?" Darian asked.

"I'm to present myself in three days."

"Three? That's not much time if it's far."

"It's far." His lips twisted. As if he had a choice. He would go, not for his sake or Samuel's. He didn't give a fuck what they did to him or the bastard who donated his seed. However, if they harmed his Doe, they'd find out just how feral this lone wolf could be.

TWENTY-SIX

WHILE THE KIDNAPPING STARTED OUT HARSH, Meadow's actual imprisonment wasn't horrible. Her abductors placed her in the tower of an actual castle. Judging by the stonework, it was centuries old at least, but upgraded. The electrical lines ran in painted conduits that ended in plugs. The plumbing had slightly larger boxing running into the small three-piece bathroom from below.

The room was large and contained a huge four-poster bed mounded in pillows plus a nightstand on either side. In front of the fireplace, which held an electric unit, were a pair of wing chairs, one covered in blue velvet, the other a multi-colored brocade.

A prison that was more luxurious than her apartment.

She'd been here two days, enough to know to

expect three meals and snacks. Good food that might result in rolling down the stairs if she stayed here too long. Exercise wasn't exactly an option unless pacing counted.

A television hung above the fireplace, with several channels to watch. Books lined the window seat. Despite that, she remained bored and lonely.

Two days here and she'd seen no one. Food came on a tray that slid through a special hatch locked within the door. She'd tried yelling at whoever delivered the meals. No reply.

Since her arrival, she'd not even seen Kit, the jerk who'd kidnapped her. This was his fault.

When she'd woken in the trunk of a car, she'd freaked and lost her mind further when his was the first face she saw upon being released from the coffin-like space.

"Bastard!" People who knew her would have been shocked at the language that spewed from her.

Did it have any effect? Kit shook his finger and tsked. "Now, now. Behave."

"Why should I? You've already told me I'm going to die."

"It's one possibility."

"What's the other?"

"That you don't."

A frustrating answer. "You must have a great

dentist. I can't even tell how many times you must have been punched in the face." A sarcastic line she'd heard Val use on many an occasion. Finally, it was Meadow's turn.

"Violence will get you nowhere."

"Says the kidnapper."

"Says the guy doing his job who'd like to be able to relax and enjoy the first-class plane ride home."

"Gonna be kind of hard to relax in cuffs after I tell everyone what you did." A plane meant people. Someone would have to listen or notice she wasn't willing.

He arched a brow. "Private plane. You'll be in cargo."

Her mouth rounded. "I'm not an animal."

"We're all animals," was his reply.

He gripped her tight by the arm and dragged her out of the trunk. She'd slapped at his hand, dug in her heels, but he still managed to get her to the plane, where another man in a uniform—indicating he was part of the flight crew—shook his head.

"You need to calm her down."

"I'm aware. You know what to do."

While Kit stood calmly, holding her one-handed, she screamed and kicked and did nothing effectual. The other man descended from the plane.

She narrowed her gaze on him. "You're abetting a crime."

The guy snorted. "You don't sign my checks." And with that, he pulled a syringe from a case and drew liquid from a bottle. Kit held her firm, arms clamped around her, meaning she couldn't escape the prick.

Next time she woke, she was strapped to a comfortable seat that hummed. Her tongue was thick, eyelids heavy.

"Where we go?" she slurred.

"Back to sleep," was the reply. Another prick in her arm dropped her back into sleep.

Who knew how long she was out. She blinked back to life in a comfortable bed.

No Kit. No phone. Nobody to ask for help. Nobody to explain. The door to the room was locked. The windows? Too high to jump from and her without Rapunzel-length hair.

The worst part had to be not knowing what they planned to do with her. Surely, they wouldn't treat her so nice if they planned to kill her. Or were these her last days?

Click.

The door finally unlocked, and she whirled. About time.

The portal opened, and there was Kit.

"You." She narrowed her gaze on the red-headed man. Handsome, if a bit sharp featured, he had strange eyes. Must be contacts.

"As pleasant as ever, I see."

"I'm sorry, did I not thank you for kidnapping me?"

"No, you didn't. Which was very unCanadian of you."

Was he trying to joke? This wasn't funny. "Release me at once."

"That's not up to me."

"Then who?" she exclaimed.

"You'll see. Follow me." He swept a hand indicating she exit, but she hesitated.

What if he was escorting her to her death?

"You going to shove me down the stairs?"

He arched a brow. "Do you really think I brought you here to do something so mundane?"

"I don't know why I'm here because no one will say anything! I demand you release me."

"Definitely not Canadian," he muttered.

"Excuse me for not enjoying my kidnapping."

"Stay here or come with me. I should note if you stay, then you won't have a chance to argue your case."

"My case of what? I didn't do anything."

"I'm not the one you need to convince. Now, are

you coming, or am I just carrying you again because you're acting like a petulant child?"

She scowled. Not a familiar expression for her. A glance down at her clothes showed where she'd spilled coffee after lunch, and had she brushed her hair today?

"One second while I freshen up." She made Kit wait while she washed her face, combed her hair, and swapped into a clean shirt. She rejoined Kit, who stood, hands shoved in his pockets, the picture of boredom.

"And she deigns to join us," he drawled. "The Council doesn't like being kept waiting."

"Then they should have given me warning."

"You had three days of contemplation."

"Try two."

"Two in the tower. The third was spent traveling."

"Unconscious."

"Ah yes, the one good day. I miss it. You were quiet." His complaint drifted behind him as he treaded lightly and quickly down the stairs. Lots of them because of the whole tower thing. Steep and tighter than she was used to seeing at home. It wouldn't be hard for her to lunge and shove him. Maybe escape.

Become a murderer...

She wasn't quite ready to make that jump. Perhaps whomever she was supposed to see would be open to releasing her.

At the bottom, a circular room offered windows covered over in vines and two hallways. He chose the one on the left, and she had to walk rapidly to keep pace. While obviously old, the castle was clean and in good repair. She could see signs of newer stonework, the hue lighter than the older original bits. The windows were modern glass, thick and draft proof.

They emerged into a grand corridor wide enough that the dark blue carpet was flanked by trees in massive stone pots. Different. Kind of nice, too. Although the bird that suddenly flitted overhead had her ducking with a sharp cry.

Kit chuckled.

"Not funny," was her grumble. "Who are we going to see anyhow?" Royalty? A castle this grand? Certainly possible. It made her wish she'd worn something a little more polished. The closet provided certainly had a wide variety of outfits. She'd gone for comfort, while Kit wore a suit. Tie, button shirt, jacket even.

"You are about to meet the most important people in the world."

"The president of the USA?" Because she

doubted the Canadian Premiere made the top tier.

"The Lykosium are above government heads. More powerful than any country's monarch, so show proper respect. You are in their world now. Abiding by their rules."

"No one is above the law."

"They are. You are in a place where democracy is but a word. The Council can decide your fate on a whim."

Great. Meeting with megalomaniac bazillionaire werewolves. Perhaps she should have stayed in her room.

Grand doors waited at the end of the long march. She half expected to see knights in clanking armor guarding them. The massive portals swung open at their approach, and they entered, Kit with a long easy stride, Meadow darting glances all around, her heart racing, her palms clammy. They wouldn't need to kill her because she might be having a heart attack.

Expecting a regal throne room, she was jarred to see instead an oasis with flowering plants around three fountains linked with babbling creeks that ran through channels in the marble floors. Pillars stretched to the high domed ceiling wrapped in leafy vines that flowered. More potted trees flourished, as did bushes and roses and flowers in wild bloom.

Apart from nature, there were benches and

sculptures by the fountains. Wolves, demi wolves, nymphs, and surely not anatomically correct men. Then again, Amarok would fit right in.

More birds flitted inside, and she'd have sworn she heard the hum of bees. What she didn't spot were any people.

Kit didn't seem perturbed. He walked toward the only sculpture not made of stone. A wooden hand that projected from the floor as if rooted there.

She thought them alone until they passed the first fat pillar. A figure, cloaked head to toe, stood there and fell in behind them, which caused her to cast more than one nervous glance over her shoulder. She could see nothing inside the cowl, but in good news, they walked upright, so not a wolf, then.

More robed figures appeared to join their procession, seven in total. Their dark garments were indistinguishable, varying only by height and girth. The shortest was a mere five feet while the tallest had to be almost eight. And she'd swear one of them glided instead of walked.

She'd entered the Twilight Zone. Or she'd fallen and banged her head good. The cause didn't matter because this couldn't be happening.

Kit stopped by the carved hand. "Sit."

She glanced around. The nearest bench was by a fountain.

"Sit." He pointed to the hand. Its palm was horizontal with its fingers raised. A strange seat and not really one she wanted to particularly try.

"I'd rather stand."

"*Sit!*"

The command could have emerged from any of the robed figures that crowded her. Arguing seemed pointless, given they outnumbered her and had proven themselves to be ruthless thus far.

It's only a chair.

She sat in the giant carved hand and almost leaped right out again as a jolt went through her. And then it was too late to flee, as the wooden fingers caged her, loosely enough she could see out, but tight enough she couldn't escape.

"What is happening?" She couldn't help but hyperventilate a bit. This wasn't normal. Wooden chairs didn't suddenly flex and move without joints or machinery. Nor were they alive.

Tell that to this sculpture.

The hooded folks spread out, ringing her. Not freaky at all.

Kit stood outside their circle, watching. In that moment, he reminded her of a fox, not just because of the red hair but his general alertness.

"State your name and address for the record," a flat voice demanded.

Record of what? This farce of a trial? "Meadow Fields, 666 Clover Lane."

Occupation. Date of arrival at the ranch. Who did she meet there? Tell them more about the beaver.

Easy stuff that wasn't exactly a secret. But then they hit the meat of the interrogation.

"What is your relationship to Amarok Fleetfoot?"

"Complicated?" she muttered. The chair vibrated, and she squirmed.

"Are you mated?" Still asked in the same even tone and yet she'd swear it came from a different robed person. Was there a person under the hood? Given everything that had happened thus far, she had to wonder.

"Why do you care if we've had sex or not?" she huffed, trying not to blush, but failing.

"Mating is more than sex. It is a binding for life that cannot be reversed."

"That's what he told me."

"And?"

She shrugged. "He said if it was meant to happen it would happen automatically."

"Did it?"

"How would I know? I was having great sex," she huffed. Still admitting too much.

"Your scent hasn't changed," a skinny robed one stated with a reedy voice.

"Says you. I'm not keen on the soap you've got the room stocked with. I kind of expected something a little more eco-friendly, less generic."

"She is avoiding answering," a short and stocky figure muttered. "Did you mate with Amarok?"

"Maybe? I mean he said he wanted me to be his, but then again, I thought he was just being romantic."

"You had sex," a different robed one stated. Slender of build. Their voice had a feminine lilt.

"Yes," she admitted, almost ducking her head in shame. This wasn't the Dark Ages. Women could go out and have sex if they wanted. With whom they wanted.

The subject abruptly shifted. "When did you first see Amarok's wolf?"

"When his dad attacked him. One minute they were fighting, and then Rok had won. He turned his back to walk away, and suddenly his father wasn't human anymore. He was a wolf. And he attacked him!"

"You saw Samuel shifting?"

"Yes." She shivered. "It was disturbing."

"And then Amarok shifted?"

"Only after his dad attacked. He pounced Rok

from behind. If anyone should be in trouble, it's Samuel. He tried to kill me, too!"

"Tell us everything that happened."

The query led to her play-by-play of the incident that ended with, "We went to his special cave. Had sex. Consensual sex," she emphasized. "I promised I wouldn't say nothing to anyone until I made some kind of promise, and when Rok left to get my dry clothes, that guy—" her gaze zeroed in on Kit—"kidnapped me."

"Kit had his orders and carried them out."

"Orders? The man drugged me. Dragged me to who knows where to meet with a bunch of crazy people in robes. And now I'm stuck in this stupid chair"—she slapped her hands against the wooden fingers—"answering questions by people too cowardly to even show their faces."

"You wish to see our faces?" The low query sent a chill through her.

"What I'd like is to not be a prisoner and for you to actually explain why I'm here."

"You're here because rules were broken."

"Rules I knew nothing about, so it hardly seems fair to judge me by them."

"Humans and your fairness." The robed figure that had led most of the interrogation snorted. "You mistake us for benevolent people. We are not. Persecution has led to us being very stringent in our dealings. Ruthless when our secrets are compromised."

"You think I'm a threat? Who would believe me? Not that I'd tell anyone," she hastily added.

"You won't. Of that we'll make sure." An ominous declaration. "Return her to the tower."

It appeared her inquisition was over. What did that mean for her? "What's going to happen to me? How long are you planning to keep me prisoner?"

"Until a verdict is reached on your case."

"Which will be how long?"

"Soon. We must confer."

"That's not an answer," she insisted as Kit grabbed her by the arm and began dragging here away.

She didn't bother fighting but had plenty to say. "How can you be a party to this?"

"The Lykosium Council does what they must to keep the Were safe."

"I'm not dangerous, though."

"That is for them to decide."

"Argh. Why must you be so annoying?"

"Why must you talk all the time?" was his reply.

"Your wife must have the patience of a saint."

"Not married."

"Probably a good thing," she muttered darkly. She'd lost her happy view on life and wondered if she'd ever get it back. Hard to be optimistic when her situation appeared so dire.

The stairs had her thighs screaming, and she was out of breath by the time she reached her room. Kit said not a word as he ushered in and locked the door.

It was only as she heard the click that her composure collapsed. Banging on the door only hurt her hand. Yelling just made her hoarse.

What would happen to her? Would she ever escape this room? And if she did, would she be alive or in a pine box?

TWENTY-SEVEN

IT DIDN'T TAKE THE FULL THREE DAYS TO GET TO Bulgaria, but it was close, given the available last-minute commercial flights. Then, from Alberta to Europe took several plane trips and twice as long. They had a nine-hour layover for mechanical failure. Then a six-hour when they landed because of an unruly passenger.

All the delays meant Rok had time to reflect on all the things he'd done wrong, starting with bringing Meadow to the hunting blind.

After the encounter with Samuel, he had wanted to be alone with her. Needed to reassure himself she'd emerged unscathed not only physically but mentally. Her discovery of the Were secret didn't just affect his relationship with her but the safety of all in his care. It was imperative he deal with the revelation quickly and without anyone butting in. His friends meant well, but Meadow was his problem. If she'd been hysterical about it... Thankfully, she'd taken it with aplomb, and everything would have worked out if some asshole hadn't stolen her.

Rok would have never ever left her if he'd known there was danger. Heck, he might have grabbed her and run if he'd known Lykosium spies lurked.

He'd thought the ranch free from their interference. They weren't a ack, just a bunch of registered loners. No big deal. If one ignored the fact their laws restricted how many Were could congregate in one place without a registered pack and a controlling Alpha.

He wasn't over by much. Maybe the enforcers sent by the Lykosium hadn't noticed. After all, they'd been more interested in Samuel.

Then why leave with Meadow? The question plagued him. The only thing that kept him from completely coming unbound was knowing she was alive. He'd claimed her. She was a part of him now. And would be until the day she died.

Which hopefully wouldn't be anytime soon.

The arrival airport for his final leg proved busy, the languages around him many and varied. He felt out of place. A Canadian on foreign shores. He'd never travelled outside of North America, and being confident didn't mean he skipped the anxiety about what would happen next.

Could he take a cab to the address given to him? Should he rent a car and drive himself?

The decision was made for him once he landed. He and his knapsack headed for the airport exit, following signs for a taxi, when his attention was caught by the appearance of a man in uniform—not the law enforcement kind but the hoity-toity staff version—holding a sign with his name.

"Hey," Rok said, approaching the guy.

It reassured to smell wolf. What didn't was the fact the guy didn't say shit. Just turned on his heel—his shoes polished and unscuffed—and led him outside. A dark sedan with tinted windows waited by the curb. The driver opened the door to the backseat. No one was there, so Rok slid inside and only had a slight moment of stress as the door shut.

Was he locked in? His fingers tensed, almost pulling at the handle to check. And if he were? Getting out wouldn't help him or Meadow. Still, he remained discomfited, not only by the tinted and soundproof windows but by the barrier between him and the driver. It proved hard not to compare the tight space to that of a coffin, albeit a luxurious one with a wet bar holding drinks and snacks.

He skipped the booze for a protein drink. He

could use the punch it packed with vitamins. Then he regretted chugging it, because what if he had to take a piss? Would the ride take minutes or hours?

He'd not dared map the route to the address beforehand knowing Reece, their computer guy, might see it. Secret was secret, and he knew someone on the ranch would have tried to follow if he had. It baffled him how he'd grown up practically friendless. Once his father took him back from his aunt, he'd rarely been allowed to see her. Or anyone for that matter. The whole caring thing didn't happen until he went to live with his uncle, who'd taught him family was who you made it, not necessarily those you shared DNA with.

Now Rok had a family, which meant a responsibility to them. He couldn't fail them or Meadow. Fuck. He hated not knowing what to expect. With no idea how long it would take, he leaned back and closed his eyes.

Exhaustion tugged. It had been a long three days. Worried about Meadow. Worried about all his friends at the ranch. Pissed that his father had returned to ruin everything good in his life.

He should have killed him when he was sixteen. Crushed that man like he'd crushed a little boy. His father was right. Being weak led to this shitshow. If only he'd killed him before chasing after Meadow, but he'd not wanted her to see the savage justice his kind employed. And now they might pay for that mistake. He wouldn't hesitate again.

Something he'd repeated a few times at the ranch as he prepared to leave.

"This is my fault. If I'd only had the balls to end this..." he'd muttered, shoving clothes into his knapsack.

"You couldn't have known the Lykosium would take Samuel into custody and that he'd rat you out," Reece reminded. He handled the booking details for Rok's trip, including locating his passport, kept in the safe they used for important documents.

"I meant I should have killed him when I had a chance as a teen."

"You were still a child," Reece pointed out.

"I stopped being a child the first time Samuel beat me."

"Let's say you had killed him back then, what would have happened?"

"I would have saved a bunch of people a shit-ton of misery."

"At what cost? You would have gone to jail."

"I probably would have gotten out by now," was his helpful reply, which led to Reece, the lease violent of them, cuffing him.

"Don't be playing the what-if game. Or the woe-

is-me shit. You made a choice. The right one at the time. Regret doesn't fix anything. We need solutions."

We. Reece used it. Lochlan. Darian. Nova... They all wanted to help.

As if Rok would let them come to possible harm. "Stay home. I'll handle this."

Much arguing ensued because every single one of them wanted to come, even the super-pregnant Astra.

"We'll handle this together. Like family."

The word hit him hard. Family didn't fuck over family. "This is my mess. I'll fix it."

"What if you can't?" Poppy's lip trembled. The little sister he'd always wanted. The one he'd sworn to protect.

His throat turned tight. "If shit goes sideways, then you should know I've got you covered. My will leaves the ranch to all of you, with Reece having controlling interest and the duty of running the day-to-day."

They'd gaped at him.

It was Nova who gasped, "You did what?"

He'd shrugged. "After my uncle died, it occurred to me that you'd all be fucked if I suddenly croaked. So I had something drawn up. It will need adjusting, obviously, as people come and go, but I wanted to be sure you always had a home." Especially since every single one of them had lost one.

It led to tears and hugs, punches with a thickly muttered, "Bastard."

His reply? "I love you, too." He went to bed that night with them planning their road trip the next morning.

By then he was already gone, and they couldn't follow. He'd made sure of that.

They were his family. It was his job to protect. He'd do anything for them.

And anything for Meadow. His mate.

He could feel the bond between them strengthening as he neared their destination. By now, those who'd taken her would know she belonged to him. The claiming would have changed her scent. Would that hurt or hinder their case?

The sedan entered a gated drive, long and winding, which led to a huge courtyard flanked on three sides by an impressively looming stone building that screamed gothic. The castle couldn't have looked more intimidating if it tried. Towers at the corners, the crenellations held slits for firing arrows. A place this age probably had a dungeon, too.

Poor Meadow. How terrified she must be. And if they'd hurt her...

With a growl, he grabbed the handle to open the car door the moment it stopped. To his surprise, it wasn't locked. He sprang from the rear seat and bounded up the steps. The door, a massive carved thing of metal, opened at his approach. No one greeted him, but it wasn't difficult to see where he should go. The wide corridor was flanked by giant potted trees, the outdoors brought in. His step quickened as he smelled her.

Meadow had passed through recently.

It took great restraint to keep himself from running. Part of the reason for his being here was for showing a lack of control. It wouldn't do to enforce that opinion.

The portal ahead swung open at his approach, and despite having never been called before the Lykosium before, he knew what to expect.

A scan of the oasis showed a man with shocking red hair standing by a robed figure. Only as he strode toward them did he notice they weren't the only ones in the room. He sensed others, hidden, waiting to reveal themselves, or were they there to ambush?

Rok wouldn't go down without a fight if they tried. He made sure to eye them all, let them know he saw them, that they didn't impress. Despite being summoned for a supposed infraction, he knew that the Were respected strength and courage.

So he swallowed that fucking anxiety and held his head fucking high.

"Sit." The man with red hair and sharp features

pointed to a hand carved from the trunk of a tree. The Hand of Truth.

He'd heard of it. People over the centuries had submitted themselves to it for interrogation. It would know if he lied. Rumor said those who fibbed in its grip never left it.

It wasn't fear but caution that made him hesitate. "Why have I been summoned?"

"Does no one follow basic instructions anymore?" grumbled the man. "What's so hard about sitting your ass down?"

"Who are you?" Although Rok was more curious to know what the man was. He reminded him strongly of fox. The same fox he'd been smelling on his land. A spy for the Lykosium. Also an impossibility. Everyone knew the Were were all wolves, no matter how many creatures movies and shows tried to create.

"Name is Kit. Happy? Now sit your ass down before I sit it for you." The man, slimmer than Rok, crossed his arms as if he thought he could actually pull off his threat.

"What are you?"

At the end of his patience, Kit stalked close and bared his teeth. "None of your fucking business."

The scent of his mate hit him hard. It covered

this man! He grabbed Kit by the shirt and snarled, "Where is Meadow?"

"None of your business."

"Oh, fuck yeah it is. You laid hands on my mate."

"Your mate?" There was a taunt in the query. "Are you sure of that?"

Rok's blood ran cold. Had he been wrong about the claiming? Had it not rooted?

"Sit." This time the command resonated from the robed figure standing in front of the carved hand. Though shorter than him, the figure emanated a vibe that Amarok knew better than to disobey.

He was in more trouble than he'd imagined. At this point, he needed to stop digging his hole of trouble any bigger. He seated himself and tried not to fidget. A man did not shy from the truth even as the fingers closed around him, trapping him. Removing his escape.

Had Meadow been subjected to it?

The interrogation started.

Name. Lineage. History.

He kept it to the simple facts. Even the part about leaving home and moving in with his uncle. He didn't make excuses as to why he left at such a young age. Were didn't whine.

He'd once heard Asher refer to the dos and don'ts of being a Were as the Nine W's.

Were didn't waiver.

Were did not walk, they ran.

Were didn't wait.

Were watched.

Were withstood all.

Were were wonderful.

Were never wept.

Were most definitely didn't whine.

And most importantly...

Were would wreak wrath upon those who wronged them.

What if Rok was the one who'd done bad, though? He knew the rules. Even agreed with their stringency. But it was hard to hold on to his composure as they began to hammer him about his father.

"When was the last time you saw you father?"

"Sperm donor or the man who truly raised me?" Because Samuel was never a real father. Rok had only ever understood what it could be like to have a home and someone who cared when he met his uncle.

"Answer the question." The robed figure didn't raise their voice. Their monotone did not give anything away, not even their sex. Odder, they had no scent. Was the robed one even Were? The only thing he could declare with any certainty was they weren't to be fucked with.

"Until a few days ago, it had been about a decade since I'd seen Samuel." Even then, he'd seen him entirely by accident. His uncle made him fly into British Columbia for a funeral. Apparently, some great-aunt on his mother's side died, and to their surprise, Samuel attended.

Rok spent the entire time waiting for a confrontation. Imagining it in his head. Planning what he'd say. Not once did Samuel try to speak with him. Nor even glance his way.

A relief and a disappointment. A part of him had wanted to confront the man.

The robed one had their hands tucked inside the sleeves. Woman? Man? Something else? "Tell us about the most recent encounter."

As if they didn't know. "Three days ago. He was skulking in the woods by my ranch. Uninvited, I should add."

"Unwelcome perhaps but not a crime since you're not in a declared pack territory," the inter-rogator remarked.

"By choice so we didn't have to deal with power-hungry Alphas." Rok didn't hold back. The system was outdated. Or at the very least corrupt when people like Samuel could be left in charge. Add in the stories from the others at the ranch and it added up to a disturbing pattern of abuse within the packs.

"You would prefer to live lawless?

"No. I understand we need rules if we're to survive among the humans. It's the Alphas who don't protect those beneath them that I have a problem with. A good Alpha should succor even the weakest, not prey upon them. Being an Alpha is not a free reign to be cruel."

"Agreed."

He startled slightly at the word. "If you agree, then why does it happen?"

"Did you file a complaint?"

He pressed his lips. "No."

"Then how is the Council supposed to know?"

"Because of your spies."

"We have limited resources to surveil the many packs."

"So you're blaming me? I was a fucking child, and you left me to be raised by a sadistic Alpha."

"How would you suggest we prevent it from happening in the future?"

"I don't know." He hated to admit they might have a point. He'd told no one of his beatings. When he was growing up, no one ever knew just how much he dreaded Samuel's temper. He'd left, and it took a while before he and his uncle ever spoke of it.

"Returning to your father. Were you aware he'd been in your area for seven days?"

A week? The shame of not realizing almost had him tucking his tail.

"How is that even possible? Someone would have smelled him. Seen him," he argued.

"There are ways of concealing presence that would account for the lack of clues."

"Is that how your spy hid?"

"Yes."

They didn't deny having him watched. "Why were you spying?"

"Recently, it was brought to our attention that a certain Alpha was abusing his role. When we sent for him, he chose to flee rather than come in for questioning."

Samuel ran. Not to escape persecution but enact one final revenge. "Which is when he came to find me and, in the process, attacked a guest of mine."

"You are referring to Ms. Fields?" the feminine voice within the hood clarified.

"Yes."

"Why did Samuel attack her? She doesn't appear to be any kind of threat."

He shrugged. "She's not. He went after her because he's nuts."

The chair gave him a jolt, and he shifted.

It was the redhead who smirked. "Are you really going to pretend you don't know?"

"Samuel attacked Meadow because she and I are involved. Given what was said, I got the impression he'd been watching us for at least a few days. When he saw an opportunity, he attacked."

"Which is when you encountered him and fought."

"I did." He fidgeted as they got to the meat of this meeting.

"During that fight, did your father shift in front of Ms. Fields?"

"Ask your spy."

"Answer the question." The robed one was firm in their demand, and he had no choice but to reply.

"Yes."

"Yes what?"

"Samuel shifted," and then because he knew he couldn't hide it, "I also changed into my wolf in order to fight him."

"In full view of Ms. Meadows." They demanded clarification.

"Yes, in front of her. He didn't leave me a choice. By that point, I knew she'd already seen everything, so rather than let him kill me, I chose to even the odds."

"The attack wouldn't have happened had you properly secured Samuel after his initial defeat at your hands." It was Kit who pointed out his lapse.

And Amarok's only excuse? "Apparently, I'm not a killer, even when it comes to assholes."

"Samuel claims you revealed yourself to the human and she was threatening to tell the world about the Were existence. He further vowed that you tried to kill him in order to cover up the fact you'd broken the rules with the very human Ms. Meadows."

Rok couldn't help it. He burst out laughing. "That is the biggest crock of bear shit I've ever heard. Did the Hand of Truth vaporize him for his lies?"

The robed one didn't reply to his query but instead said, "Why would Samuel fabricate such a story?"

"The man is a sadistic psycho who suddenly decided he needed to fuck up my life because it was going well."

"According to you."

"According to anyone who has a discussion with the fucker." Forget holding his temper.

"Samuel was interviewed."

"So you know he's a fucking liar then."

Kit snorted. "We know. Knew the moment the Hand of Truth fisted shut and refused to let him sit."

The robed one moved their discussion along. "Is Ms. Fields Oathbound?"

"Not yet. Things happened kind of quickly after

Samuel's attack. But she did promise me she wouldn't tell, and it was our plan to have her taken to an Alpha to pledge, only someone stole her before we could act." His gaze slewed to Kit.

"If it's any consolation, she did declare you'd come for her," Kit announced.

"You fucker. You took her!" The man confirmed it, and Rok wanted to punch that smug expression. The chair held him in place.

"Kit. No antagonizing him," the robed one chided.

"What's he gonna do? Prove he's a feral like his father and attack?" Kit mocked.

Rok ignored the taunting to argue his case. "Meadow didn't do anything wrong. She was going to swear to an Alpha soon as we got to the city. Another day and it would have been done."

"Kit did move a tad quickly. But circumstance and all that. There was concern once we became aware of the situation."

"Well, he should have tried talking to me first. He took my mate."

"*Is* she your mate, though?"

This was the second time Kit implied she wasn't. Had his claim not taken? Could they not smell it? It would hurt his argument if they thought she wouldn't bind with him. "Meadow and I are fated. I knew it from the moment we met."

"Yet you initially told her to leave," the robed one stated.

Shit, they were well informed. "I changed my mind."

"Why did it need changing if she was your mate?" Flatly asked and yet he heated.

"Because I'm a dumbass, okay? I met her and knew she was someone special and it scared the fuck out of me." The chair didn't singe his ass, and he'd have sworn he felt satisfaction from the robed figure. Before they could ask about the claiming, he returned to a more pressing subject. "Where is Samuel now?" Did he need to warn the ranch? What about Meadow? Was she safe from him?

"Samuel is not your problem."

"It is a problem if he's loose. He poses a danger to everyone associated with the ranch."

"Ah, yes, the ranch your uncle left you. Glad you mentioned it, as that is a major area of concern. You currently have many Were in residence."

"Yes." No point in lying.

"There are rules against more than eight Were congregating in one location outside a pack." It was meant to prevent unsanctioned wolf packs from forming.

"It just kind of happened. They needed a place to go. We couldn't turn them away."

"Those rules exist for a reason."

"To avoid notice, I get it, but we literally live in the backwoods. There's no one else around."

"And yet a human managed to stumble upon the Were secret."

"Because Samuel wanted to cause trouble."

"And then you compounded it by shifting yourself," the robed one hammered.

But he wouldn't bend. "I chose to not die." Which was contrary to what was expected. Death before revelation. "Once Samuel shifted, there was no point in keeping the secret."

"And so you told her everything?"

"She swore she'd never reveal what she discovered, and I believe her."

"But you're not an Alpha," Kit reminded, with a sneer. "Just a feral hick."

Rok said nothing because any reply would show how the barb struck.

The robed one dismissed him. "We've heard enough. You will leave us while we ruminate on your fate."

As if he'd go without asking. "I want to see Meadow."

"Demands in your position? You're either very brave or phenomenally stupid," taunted Kit.

"She's my mate. We belong together." He remained firm on that point.

The robed one nodded. "Take him to her. Might as well allow them this night together while we decide their fate."

Ominous and yet he didn't care. He was finally going to be reunited with his Doe.

Hopefully, she didn't hate him after all that had happened.

TWENTY-EIGHT

I HATE WAITING.

There was little to do in her tower room other than worry. Meadow had spent the time since her meeting with the creepy robed people pacing and wondering what would happen to her. The questions had been so odd. Had she answered right? Wrong? Did she get Rok and the others in trouble?

She hoped not, because she got the impression these people didn't mess around. Just look at what they'd done to her thus far. Only ruthless people kidnapped. And given she'd seen Kit's face, did that mean they didn't plan to let her go?

Pace. Pace. Her agitation had trebled in the last hour, and thoughts of Rok kept bombarding her. Her whole body prickled, and she kept glancing over her shoulder as if expecting to see him.

Then suddenly, she stopped moving and stared at her door. She wasn't surprised when someone knocked.

"You've got a visitor," Kit yelled through the portal, his voice muffled.

"Go away!" She had no interest in talking to that red-headed psycho.

"Doe, it's me."

Her jaw hit the floor as she froze with her mouth open.

Rok came for me!

She darted for the door as it was unlocked and opened.

Rok's body took up the whole frame, his face a thundercloud. His eyes brightened at the sight of her.

"Rocky!" she squealed. A second later, she was in his arms, wrapped tight.

He hugged her close, nuzzling her cheek. The portal shut and locked, but neither paid any mind.

"Thank fuck, you're okay," he murmured.

"For now," she grumbled. "The world's freakiest people said something about deciding my fate."

"Would it help if I told you they said the same about mine?"

"We're in big trouble, aren't we?" She glanced up at him.

"We are, even as we shouldn't have been. It is their fault we didn't have time to get you Oathbound."

He spoke of that pledge she was supposed to make. "I told them I promised you."

"I'm not an Alpha, which means it didn't count."

"It's their fault given they kidnapped me before we could find one."

"I did point that out." Rok traced a strand of hair from her cheek to her ear. "I told them you'd be willing to pledge and blamed that red-headed fucker for acting too fast."

"No kidding. I could have used a few days alone with you before getting abducted."

"I'd prefer you weren't taken at all." He scrubbed a hand through his hair and moved away from her to pace in agitation.

"Are you going to stress about something that's already happened or make my possible final hours a little more pleasurable?"

He blinked at her.

She grabbed hold of his jacket and yanked him close. "I've been locked in this room for three days. I don't know what tomorrow will bring, but I do know what I'd like right now."

"We really should talk." His weak attempt to be responsible.

Meadow wasn't in the mood. "After. Right now, I'd really like it if you at least pretended you were happy to see me." Because he was scowling mighty fierce. Sure, he'd come for her, but he didn't seem too crazy about it.

"Of course, I'm happy to see you, Doe. Do you have any idea of the things I thought might have happened?" He pushed Meadow away at arm's length, only so he could inspect her.

"They didn't hurt me. Although that Kit is no gentleman."

"You don't say. I met the arrogant, spying bastard," he growled.

"Sounds about right."

"I'm thinking I'll challenge him."

"You'll what?"

"Challenge Kit to a fight. It's an honor thing."

"How about instead of plotting revenge we plot escape?"

"We can't escape. They'd hunt us down and kill us for sure."

"Meaning we wait for a verdict." She smiled. "I know what we can do to pass the time." She grabbed him, cupping his groin.

He leaned his hips into her touch. "I missed you."

"Missed you more," she teased.

"Doubtful." He dragged her upward for a kiss, a hard slash of his mouth that stole her breath.

He kept on nipping and teasing her mouth as he went after her gown, yanking it up and only taking his mouth away long enough to pull it off completely. Leaving her naked. Which was when she attacked his clothes. Stripped his delicious body with its ridges. Licked and bit at him even as he did the same to her.

They came together in a passionate clash of bodies that barely made it to the bed. Their touch was frantic, their breaths even more rough.

He touched her. His fingers were rough, but her body craved it. He slid a digit into her slick pussy, and she growled, "I want you. Now." She was ready and needed the thick feel of him.

He didn't argue. He pressed his tip against the mouth of her sex, stretching her, giving her something to clamp down on.

The deep thrust led to a sense of fullness. The grind pushed against her sweet spot inside. As he moved, he gave her what she needed. Filled a spot inside her she'd not known was hollow. She felt that connection he'd alluded to. That shining moment where she saw him clearly and realized he was the other part of her.

"Rok." She panted his name.

"Doe," he murmured right back.

Together they rocked in rhythm until their climax hit, a moment so perfect, so right, she wanted to float in it forever.

Although coming back down, wrapped in his arms, her head resting on his chest, was pretty nice, too.

They didn't say much, but they made love again before sleeping. And when they woke.

And in the shower.

Still, she craved him. Was aware of him in a way she'd never imagined.

Mated. A word that now made sense to her, even as she was terrified by it. Because they both knew, at any moment, some faceless strangers might wreck it.

They were dressed and ready when, after the delivered breakfast, they were summoned.

She took a shuddering breath, whereas Rok put a hand in the middle of her back and said, "Don't worry. I won't let anyone hurt you."

That was all well and good for her, but what if someone tried to hurt him?

TWENTY-NINE

THE WALK UP THE HALL WAS BOTH MORE AND less stressful at the same time. Rok had his mate by his side. Her claimed scent was unmistakable this morning. Her trusting smile as they ventured into the unknown was the most precious thing in the world.

Given how they'd been treated, he no longer believed the Lykosium would harm them. After all, Meadow never had a chance to talk to anyone, and now that she was truly his mate, it would be a simple matter to get her oathbound, making the Were secret safe.

Or so he kept trying to convince himself. Ultimately, the Lykosium would decide, not him. He could only hope they were reasonable—and didn't believe his father's lies.

The garden oasis appeared as before, but rather than have them sit in the Hand of Truth, they were led to a table with four chairs. A seat was already occupied by a slender robed one, hard to tell which one from the day before. Kit eschewed sitting to stand behind, hands behind his back, looking casual and yet obviously on guard.

"Sit," the robed one said before revealing themselves. A woman with dark, smooth skin and amber eyes. She could have been any age with her lack of wrinkles, but her experienced gaze indicated older rather than younger. She didn't smile as she dipped her head and said, "I am Luna."

"Like the goddess," Rok replied and seated Meadow before himself, wondering if the fact a council member chose to show her face was a good or bad thing.

"Exactly like the goddess." Spoken deadpan. She cocked her head. "You are both curious to know our decision."

"Very much," Meadow exclaimed. Her fingers laced with his on the table.

Luna's gaze drifted to their clasped hands for a moment. "There was some arguing as to your fate, especially given the number of rules broken. Some which were admittedly out of your control. Which is why on the matter of Ms. Fields being exposed to our culture, we find Amarok Fleetfoot not guilty."

He relaxed.

"Now onto the charge of Ms. Meadows knowing of our secret and not having pledged to a declared alpha."

"Because we weren't given time," Rok grumbled.

"Which was taken into consideration. It's been noted that, since her discovery of the Were existence, Ms. Fields hasn't had time to speak to anyone, meaning there is still an option for her to refuse the pledge."

"What? Since when?" he blurted out. "All humans who know our secret must take the Oath. It's law."

"A law with some flexibility that few know about. Should she choose not to pledge, it is possible to wipe her memories of meeting you and her time at your ranch."

"Wipe them?" Meadow was the one to shake her head before he could roar. "But I don't want to forget."

Luna's eyes swirled for a moment, as if many colors at once, before steadying. "It would seem that is no longer an option given the claiming has manifested since our last meeting."

"Given the fact we're mated, and only the Oath

stands in our way, then let her pledge to you, here and now," Rok demanded.

"Can I?" Meadow asked, glancing at him first then Luna. "Because I will solemnly swear to keep your secrets. Cross my heart and swear I'll die if I break that promise."

Luna's staid demeanor didn't crack one bit but remained serious as she said, "You do realize the mating and Oath bind you for life. You cannot change your mind. This is forever."

Meadow being Meadow kept talking. "I understand, and while I know it's crazy, it's also the most exciting thing to ever happen to me. Meeting Rok has been life changing, and I don't mean just because of the wolf thing. He's that happily-ever-after romance I've been fantasizing about. A thing I didn't actually believe could be real until I met him."

Her smile at him had him feeling all kinds of things, including protective, which might explain his growl as Luna tried to convince his mate otherwise.

"You say that but have yet to realize the difference it will make in your life. The secrets you'll have to keep from your old friends and family."

She shrugged. "At one point in everyone's life, we grow up and move on. We get into relationships that take us new places. And the secrets we keep from our old life are what binds us to the new."

He blinked at Meadow and blurted out, "That was some sage fucking shit."

Her cheek dimpled as she grinned. "I like to read self-help books."

"There is no book on being the mate of a Were," Luna pointed out.

"But there are people I can talk to. Like Rok and Nova and Astra. Even you, if you give me your number so we can chat."

Kit snickered even as Rok couldn't believe Meadow said it. More astonishing, Luna almost smiled.

"Aid transitioning can be provided if requested, although I do believe you'll be fine," said the other woman.

"Awesome. So when and to whom should I pledge?" Meadow appeared eager to do so even as she argued. "Although I don't see what the difference is between me promising Rok and telling a stranger. I mean I'm more likely to mean it when I tell Rok I would never do anything that would harm him." She smiled in his direction, and he felt himself reacting to the truth of her statement.

"I am going to be sick," Kit complained. "I hate the newly mated."

"Only because it hasn't happened to you yet," chided Luna.

"Hmph," was the grumpy man's reply.

"I do have a question, though," Meadow said. "Does this mating mean no white dress or cake smashing? Because I know my mom's been holding on to her veil for me and my dad always thought he'd get to give me away."

Rok would give her anything she wanted if they got out of this fucking mess. "We can get married any way you like, but I draw the line at the wasting of cake."

"Good point. Cake is precious."

"Ahem." They eyed the throat-clearing Luna. "I haven't rendered my decision."

"We'd be dead already if it was bad," was Rok's drawled reply.

Luna definitely had a lip twitch that time. "It is our ruling that the vow Meadow Fields made to you is binding and the claiming verified. As such, Ms. Fields is free to depart."

"Yay!" she cheered and threw her arms around him.

He hugged her back, even as a part of him knew this wasn't over. Luna hadn't said he could leave, too.

"You are excused." Luna dismissed Doe, her swirling gaze fixed on Amarok.

Meadow stood, only to realize he didn't. "Rok?"

"Mr. Fleetfoot will be along shortly. He and I need to speak a bit further."

"No. I won't leave without him," Meadow insisted stubbornly.

"Would it help if I promised he won't come to any harm? Just a quick chat and then he'll be yours."

Meadow chewed her lip before nodding.

He stood and drew her close for a kiss, whispering, "Start planning that wedding because it's happening soon as we get home."

"We might need a little longer than that to plan," was her laughed reply, which didn't quite dispel all her anxiety.

Meadow left with Kit, and Rok found himself alone with Luna. What did she have to say? He could only assume this had to do with Samuel.

He was wrong.

"Now to deal with the issue of your pack."

"I don't have a pack." His heart raced because he knew there were harsh penalties for illegal packs.

"Don't you? My eyes and ears claim there are twelve wolves living on your ranch, including you. Thirteen now with Meadow. Fourteen once the baby is born."

Rok cleared his throat. "You should subtract one, as Samuel killed one of the older Weres."

Luna waved a hand. "Which still leaves you well over the eight mark."

A wince tugged Rok's features. He knew he'd been stretching the rules, but how could he turn anyone away? "Guess I'll have to ask some of them to find a new place." Which killed him, because how could he choose?

Once more, Luna tilted her head and freaked him out with her eyes. "Why do that? Did it never occur to you to apply for permission to form a pack?"

"Not really." He'd lived in a pack and had no interest in doing so again.

"Why not?" Luna asked. "It would solve your issue and allow you to take in more loners."

"You're forgetting one thing. A pack needs an Alpha, and I'm not about to let an outsider come in and take over my uncle's ranch or start abusing folks like my father did."

"Understandable, but why would you bring in a stranger when you already have a suitable Alpha?"

He frowned. "Who?" Reece was pretty organized but shit when it came to discipline. Gary was too shy. Bellamy could keep shit in order, as could Darian, but neither showed an inclination to lead. Could be Nova. Female Alphas were rare but not unheard of.

Didn't matter who. If the ranch had a candidate,

then forming a pack would be an ideal solution. He trusted everyone already so wouldn't have to worry about being ousted from his own home, and they wouldn't have to worry about needing an outsider for pledges. They could even offer sanctuary to more outcast Weres needing a place they could fit in.

"You really haven't the slightest clue." Luna clucked her tongue. "You, Amarok Fleetfoot. You are the Alpha."

He digested the words and then laughed. "Nope."

"Yes. Or haven't you noticed that you're already leading a pack? Making the decisions. Keeping your people safe and in line."

He opened his mouth and shut it. Frowned. "Just making sure we keep our heads down and get to live without any bullshit."

"What do you think being an Alpha is?"

"I thought an Alpha was someone nominated by the Lykosium Council."

"In some cases, where there isn't a clear choice, then yes, we'll have a hand in selection, but most packs nominate their Alphas and then just ask for approval."

"If the pack usually chooses, then shouldn't we be asking the folks at the ranch what they think? You can't just make me their boss."

"And if I said they already agreed?"

"I'd have to ask when because no one said shit about talking to you guys about it." Then again, most kept their business with the Lykosium quiet.

"You have very loyal friends. The sign of a strong pack. They've contacted us, arguing your case and Meadow's."

His brows lifted. "Those idiots were supposed to let me handle it! I didn't want them involved."

"It must be horrible to be so well regarded," Luna mocked.

It brought a wry smile to his lips. "Not much of an Alpha I guess since they didn't listen."

"Actually, the fact they cared says more about you than you apparently realize. Wasn't it you that claimed an Alpha should put the needs of his pack ahead of his own and protect those weaker than him?"

"Yes."

"Like you've already been doing that."

He grimaced. "Just doing what was right."

"And now the Council is going to give you the power to keep doing so." Luna stood, and he scrambled to follow suit.

She kept her hood down and was joined by more people in robes. He might have gotten nervous if she'd not said, "Amarok Fleetfoot, kneel and give oath."

What oath? He had no idea what she meant even as he hit the floor on his knees. He stared at the stone floor, and as the silence stretched, the waiting kind that wanted him to speak, the words came to him.

"I solemnly swear to lead my pack honestly, fairly, and to protect them from all harm. To keep their secret. Succor them in times of need. And to never abuse them or let them be abused. So long as I live." The moment he stopped speaking it hit him. Not with a slap or a jolt but a sense of rightness in his heart and soul.

Luna smiled. "Rise Alpha. You no longer kneel to anyone."

He was about to reply when he was hit with a sense of wrongness. He eyed the closed door to the chamber before sprinting for it.

Meadow was in trouble.

THIRTY

MEADOW FOLLOWED KIT OUT OF THE WEIRD garden room, alternating between happiness and worry. She glanced over her shoulder often, looking for Rok.

As she stalled at the entrance to the tower, Kit sighed. "He's fine."

"How would you know?"

"Because I do."

"Then why did I have to leave?" It emerged poutier than she liked.

"Were matters. No humans allowed."

She rolled her eyes. "Why not just say that in the first place?"

"Because we don't have to explain ourselves." His grumpy reply.

Eyeing his flame-red hair, on impulse she asked, "Are you a fox? Or a wolf?"

"How about none of your business."

"It was you I saw that day on the other side of the creek, though. Watching us?"

No reply.

"I showed the picture to Rok, and he thought it was fake because fox and wolf hybrids are impossible."

"Guess again." A surprise reply.

"So you are both? How? Did you get it from your parents?"

They were beginning the ascent to her room when he half turned to snarl, "Enough of the—"

Kit dropped suddenly, his body slumping in the stairs. The reason why stepped over it as he rounded the curve.

Samuel smiled. "And we meet again, whore."

Panic filled her as she whipped around and bolted. She hit the ground floor and would have run to the throne room, only Samuel leaped to stand in front. Smirking. His eyes carried a wild light.

Her tongue got stuck, as did the scream in her chest.

Samuel sniffed, only once, and grimaced. "He fucking mated you. After I told him not to waste his time. Guess it's a good thing I'm here to fix his mistake."

She backed away. "Leave me alone."

"Or what? You'll cry? It's the only thing humans are good at. Weak. Inferior. Just like his mother. I should have known better than to mate with her defective ass. Look at what she died birthing."

"Rok is a good man."

"Good is another word for sniveling coward." Samuel advanced on her, and for each step he took, she managed two back.

Where was everyone? Did this place have any guards? She'd yet to see any. If she screamed, would anyone even come?

"You going to run and make this fun?" Samuel taunted.

"You're insane."

"Actually, the correct term is feral. It's what happens when an Alpha becomes unbound from his pack and has nothing to tether him. Not mate. Not family. Nothing to lose." His teeth flashed.

Her stomach clenched in fear.

A door shut in the distance. Samuel glanced at the stairwell, and while he was turned, she conquered her freezing terror to bolt out the door.

Once outside, she had no idea where to go. The day was dark with storm clouds. The wind whipping. She was in a foreign country with a rabid wolf after her ass.

Before she could run, Samuel was there. He grabbed hold of her hair and yanked, drawing a sharp cry.

Rescue arrived.

"Unhand her." Amarok's voice had a steely vein in it that had Samuel uttering a nasty chuckle.

"Should have known you'd come running for your whore." Samuel turned and dragged Meadow around with him.

Rok stood in front of the castle. She blinked. Knowing she'd been inside one and seeing it were two different things. Vlad the Impaler could have been at home here, but instead she was caught between a feral werewolf and the one who loved her.

"Whatcha going to do? Beg for her life? Offer your own in exchange?" Samuel taunted.

"You can have a quick death or a slow one." Rok cocked his head and offered a cold smile. "I know which one I'd prefer."

It should have shocked her, but there was a strange satisfaction at hearing his threat.

"Finally growing some balls, boy."

"That's Alpha to you," Rok declared.

That caused Samuel to jerk with a start. "I ain't dead yet, and even if I were, my pack belongs to someone else because of those fuckers." He aimed the last at the robed figures standing sentinel at Rok's back, watching. Waiting.

"Shall we end this?" Rok asked.

Rather than reply, Samuel shoved Meadow. She hit the ground on her hands and knees, drawing a sharp cry.

Rok let out a howl and he grabbed his shirt and tugged. He threw his head back as he tore and changed into a beautiful white wolf, massive in size, much more intimidating than the scraggly gray facing off against him.

In that moment, Samuel came to his senses, or at least self-preservation kicked in. Rather than fight, he bolted for the woods, but not before slamming into Meadow and tearing a gash along her arm!

"Ow." She hissed in pain, slapping a hand over the wound.

She expected Rok to go after him, but her mate instead came over to nose her. While he didn't chase, others did, including a massive fox with wolf traits.

Amarok shifted and knelt. "Give me your arm."

It throbbed and bled, enough that the sight of it made her dizzy. In a second, Amarok was behind her supporting and then lifting her to carry her inside.

"Bring her to the tower and we'll bind it." She recognized Luna's voice.

"Shouldn't you be out there hunting Samuel?" she asked as Rok kept her cradled in his arms.

It was Luna who said, "Samuel is our problem now. We'll handle it."

The cut itself didn't take long to fix. Luna applied a salve and a bandage, which a servant brought. Luna didn't linger, leaving her alone with a naked Amarok.

"What happened after I left?" she asked. "You said you're an Alpha now? Isn't that like a wolf leader?"

His lips curved. "It is. I'm now officially in charge of the Weres at the ranch."

"Which is a good thing?"

"I guess. It will give me the ability to better protect and allow me to help others who might need a place to stay."

"Because you have a big heart." She reached out to him, and he drew her into his arms.

"Only a big heart?" he teased.

"You going to show me something else that's big?" She tilted her lips for a kiss. He didn't disappoint.

While the kiss was fraught with passion, his touch was gentle, too soft, which was why she had to growl, "Stop taunting me and fuck me."

The vulgar words had him giving her what she

needed. What she wanted, until they both lay together, basking in the afterglow.

"What happens now?" she asked, lying splayed across his chest.

"Time we went home."

THIRTY-ONE

A private jet, owned by the Lykosium, took them home. They arrived at the ranch to everyone huddled on the porch, faces drawn with worry. Fearful and, at the same time, cautiously optimistic. After all, Rok had returned alive with Meadow, but they didn't yet know the other news. He'd only given Reece a quick shout to let him know they were on their way.

Rok was still stepping out of his truck when Nova exclaimed, "What happened?"

Eyeing them, his people, he couldn't help a huge burst of love and pride as he said, "The Lykosium have declared us pack and me your Alpha. Which I know is a big change and might not be cool with some of you. I get it. If you want to go, I won't hold you back, but if you stay—"

"Shut the fuck up," Nova exclaimed. "None of us are going anywhere."

"We're really pack?" Astra held her belly, and her eyes shone. Being an official pack meant she didn't have to worry about them losing their home. Or that their child might grow up without the protection of its kind.

"I'm cool with it," Asher declared. "But what's our pack name? Because I thought there was already a White Wolf Pack."

"There is."

"So what's our name then?" Poppy asked.

And this was where Rok winced. "So, I might have fucked that part up."

"What did you do?" Darian asked.

Meadow giggled. "He got drunk."

"A certain red-headed fucker wouldn't stop calling me a feral hick, and after a few too many beers, we made a wager, which I lost."

"We're the Feral Hick Pack?" Nova grimaced.

"Feral Pack actually," he corrected somewhat sheepishly. And once the Alpha declared it, apparently, there was no taking it back.

It was Poppy who clapped her hands and said, "It's perfect, because we'll go rabid on anyone who ever tries to harm us."

Lochlan actually chuckled. "You know what, it

does kind of suit us. I mean, we've all seen what happens when Poppy makes her special brownies and it's every person for themselves."

"Reminds me of Darian when someone doesn't check the oil in the ATV before taking it out and getting it stuck," Hammer offered.

"Me, when I'm PMSing," Nova volunteered.

Rok shook his head as his damned pack took the bungle he'd made of their name and turned it into something good. "You're all fucking idiots."

"Your idiots," Astra stated proudly.

And he loved them all, especially his mate. Which was why, when she asked after dinner to check on Weaver, he held her hand as they picked their way up the path.

As his mate exclaimed over the fact the beaver appeared to have rebuilt his dam in the week they'd been gone, he turned his head at a crackle in the woods.

He frowned even as he saw and scented nothing.

"What's wrong?" Meadow asked.

"Nothing. Let's go home. We have a wedding to plan." And the rest of their lives to look forward to.

OUT OF SIGHT, Kit—who'd been led on a merry chase—kept the pressure on Samuel's throat. His lips were close to the man's ear as he whispered, "You should have never come back here."

Samuel might have replied if Kit hadn't snapped his neck and done the world a favor.

EPILOGUE

TURNED OUT BEING ALPHA JUST INVOLVED doing the same as before, but with his friends adding a teasing, "Yes, Alpha," every time Rok made a request.

He'd have reamed them about it except for the fact he could hear the joy in their voices each time they said it.

The wedding preparations were underway and planned for a month from now, when the fall would have the leaves turning. Meadow spent a lot of time on the phone that first week with her parents and her best friend, who wasn't crazy about Meadow's sudden jump into matrimony.

"Val's protective about me," Meadow confided as they snuggled in bed.

"Not as much as I am," he growled.

"Oh, Rocky."

"What did I say about calling me that?"

"Oops," she giggled. Happy all the time, the way a mate should be. Would be. Now and forever. Or so help him, he'd fucking go feral on someone's ass.

THE NEXT DAY...

There was a mighty pounding at the door, and Asher, currently helping himself to one of Poppy's epic cupcakes, debated answering it. Last time a stranger came knocking, their new Alpha got mated.

What if answering the door was the equivalent of catching the bouquet?

"You gonna answer that?" Lochlan groused from his spot at the table.

"Why don't you?"

"Because I don't like people."

Asher frowned. "I do, usually, but that's some angry knocking."

"Yup."

Asher moved to the hall and stared at the solid wood door, nervous, which wasn't like him.

"Open this door before I call the cops!" hollered

a woman. "Meadow! You in there? I've come to rescue you."

Asher's brows rose as he headed for the door and swung it open to see a tall brunette with flashing angry eyes.

"Where's Meadow?" snapped the stranger.

"Around here somewhere."

"Are you Amarok?"

"Who's asking?"

"Her best friend, Val, asshole. What have you done with her?"

Asher eyed Val up and down. Her heaving bosom. Her flushed cheeks. The shaking fist.

Mine, oh, mine.

Uh-oh.

SPARKS ARE ABOUT TO FLY, **so stayed tuned for the next book in Feral Pack, Beta Untamed.**

MORE INFO AT EVELANGLAIS.COM.

Made in the USA
Coppell, TX
07 November 2022